# KEEP YOUR FRIENDS CLOSE

# KEEP YOUR FRIENDS CLOSE

## THE KURTHERIAN ENDGAME™ - OUT OF TIME
### BOOK ONE

### ND ROBERTS

### MICHAEL ANDERLE

DISRUPTIVE IMAGINATION

Copyright © 2019 N.D. Roberts and Michael Anderle
Cover by Andrew Dobell, www.creativeedgestudios.co.uk
Cover copyright © LMBPN Publishing
Interior Images by Eric Quigley
Interior Images © LMBPN Publishing
This book is a Michael Anderle Production

LMBPN Publishing
PMB 196, 2540 South Maryland Pkwy
Las Vegas, NV 89109

First US edition, September, 2019
eBook ISBN: 978-1-64202-446-3
Print ISBN: 978-1-64202-447-0

KEEP YOUR FRIENDS CLOSE TEAM

**Thanks to our Beta Readers:**
Diane Velasquez, Dorene Johnson, USNR, and
Timothy Cox

**Thanks to the JIT Readers**

Dave Hicks
Dorothy Lloyd
Misty Roa
Peter Manis
John Ashmore
Deb Mader
Micky Cocker
Diane L. Smith
Jeff Eaton
James Caplan
Larry Omans
Jackey Hankard-Brodie

*If I've missed anyone, please let me know!*

**Editor**
Lynne Stiegler

# DEDICATION

*For the children we all are in our hearts.*

*— Nat*

*To Family, Friends and*
*Those Who Love*
*To Read.*
*May We All Enjoy Grace*
*To Live The Life We Are*
*Called.*

*—Michael*

**Devon, The Hexagon, Private Elevator**

"There's a vault down here, and a lab? When was all of this even built?" K'aia shifted her weight onto her back legs and craned around Michael's shoulders to get a view of the elevator panel.

Her expression grew more suspicious at the lack of buttons to press. "There's no indication in the security manual that the floor we're going to exists."

"Take it easy, K'aia," Michael cautioned gently. "This part of the Hexagon is completely isolated from network command and CEREBRO."

"ADAM is the only digital entity with access besides Eve," Bethany Anne confirmed. She chuckled at the young Yollin's gaping mandibles. "All the better to hide you all from those who wouldn't think twice about using you four to get to us."

"Some of whom include Tu'Reigd's family," Michael reminded them. "Do not forget that. The only thing that swayed us from choosing the High Tortuga base was that the vault is comparably secure."

Bethany Anne nodded in agreement. "More, if you consider all the extras we had Eve put in. There is nothing more precious to us than you," she told all four solemnly. "We would go to any lengths to keep you safe while we fight for Qu'Baka's freedom."

Gabriel rolled his eyes reflexively. "We should be going with you, not hiding in an underground cell."

Bethany Anne raised an eyebrow. "It's hardly a cell. You will be in the gameworld, which, and please correct me if I'm wrong, is your favorite place to be."

Gabriel shrugged, his disappointment clear in his posture. "In my downtime, yeah. There's only so far Vid-doc training goes. We'll still have to spend time syncing our bodies with our neurological gains when we get out."

Michael understood his son's disappointment. "Wait until you get into the training program before you decide where you would rather be. Alexis, you especially will be intrigued by the mechanics of the gameworld." He smiled at his daughter's interested expression, dropping his voice to a conspiratorial whisper. "Your curiosity about the nano-curtain technology is about to be satisfied."

Alexis smiled pensively. "I appreciate that, Dad. But I don't have to like that you and Mom sprang this on us with no warning." The unexpected family dinner after the gala had distracted her and Gabriel both, and this morning their mother was walking an emotional tightrope that she and her brother were in perfect agreement they had no wish to trip. "You could tell us what scenario we're heading into."

Bethany Anne lifted her hands. "There wasn't much time to get everything ready. Eve has prepared a briefing for you."

Alexis shared a furtive glance with Gabriel, then aired her concern. "Is this our punishment for trashing the *Izanami?*"

Michael smiled, placing a hand on each of the twins' shoulders. "The punishment for hijacking your mother's favorite ship and crashing it is that the two of you will remain here instead of accompanying us to Qu'Baka as planned."

Gabriel folded his arms and leaned against the wall in sullen silence.

Bethany Anne's tolerance for sulking usually ran in the minus. This was different. "ADAM, stop the elevator." She took Gabriel's shoulder and turned him to face her. "Dammit, when are you going to stop getting taller? Listen carefully. This started out as an object lesson, but not because we were angry with you."

She looked Alexis and Gabriel in the eyes. "You're not little kids anymore. I get that. But you are *not* adults. Far from it. You could have been killed just feet from my position, and there would have been nothing I could do to save you."

"You were trapped inside that factory!" Gabriel found the denial leaving his mouth before he knew it was coming.

Alexis was quick to agree. "I'm sorry, Mom, but what were we supposed to do?"

Bethany Anne held up a finger to cut off the twins' protests. "You were *supposed* to remain on Devon like your father and I told you to. Hmmm?" Her face softened slightly at their hangdog expressions. "I know you acted, thinking you had to save me. It was noble, and I'm proud of you for having the courage. But it wasn't necessary. You are not ready to be out there with us, and we nearly lost Izanami because of it."

Neither of them could argue with that.

"I want us all to be crystal-clear on this." Bethany Anne waved a finger to include K'aia. "This is the conclusion of your education. It's not a game. You are not being distracted while we 'take care of the adult stuff.' We are providing the four of you the opportunity to live. To grow, and make choices of your own. That's something we and Mahi' believe has been denied to you all because of your status as our children."

"This is your chance to make those choices without the consequences affecting the lives of millions," Michael clarified. "That's a luxury few in your position are afforded. ADAM, let's get this over with."

K'aia gazed up wistfully when the elevator started moving again. "I'm not destined to lead anyone, thankfully, but that's life. You go where it takes you, even if that's into a freaking video game for the next six years."

"We would not separate the four of you for any amount of time," Michael told her. "It is already hard enough to leave you behind."

Alexis almost broke into sobs at the uncharacteristic display of emotion from her father, but she kept her peace. Separation was difficult for all of them as a family, but when their parents had a war to win, there was no justification for making it worse.

Still, Alexis was in an elevator she hadn't known existed, heading deeper below the Hexagon than she had known was possible. She felt like a little girl on her first day at school, which made the realization that the next time she used this elevator, she would be an adult woman all the more jarring. When they got out of the Vid-docs, the fight for Qu'Baka would be over, and Trey would leave to rule his people.

Gabriel reached out over their mental link to comfort Alexis, his own grumbles seeming somewhat shallow to him after brushing up against his sister's turmoil. *It's only a few years in game-time. We know we're coming home at the end, and by then, there won't be any reason for us to stay back when Mom and Dad go out to fight.*

Alexis smiled, appreciating his effort. *I know, but Trey's our friend. I feel like we should be doing more to help him get his home back.*

*I'm pretty sure we're gonna find out Trey feels the same way when we get to the vault,* Gabriel assured her. He supposed some might think it a curse to know how others were feeling, but he considered it a blessing to have the ability to brighten his sister's perspective with a thought. *This is what we've got to work with, and we have to at least* try *to be okay with it.*

*I know,* Alexis conceded. *Suck it up; you're right. Mom's not finding this easy at all. We can't make it worse for her.*

Bethany Anne wasn't blind to the mixed emotions coming from Alexis and Gabriel. She pulled them to her and pressed a kiss to each of their foreheads in turn. "I'm going to miss you both. I know it won't be as long for us as it will be for you, but you can message us as much as you want."

"What about the time dilation?" K'aia asked. "Won't that mean a crap-ton of messages every time you check? How about real-time interactions like vid-calls?"

"Eve fixed the dilation problem *ages* ago." Alexis wrapped her arms around Bethany Anne and squeezed. "I'm going to miss *you*, Mom." She let go and turned to hug Michael. "I'm going to miss you too, Dad. It feels like we're leaving home."

Michael cleared his throat, suddenly finding it difficult to speak around the lump that had formed there at the thought of his children living their own lives, separate from him and Bethany Anne. "In a way, I suppose you are. It is natural for a person coming of age to strive for room to grow."

Bethany Anne held back her tears. She wiped her eyes with a sniff. "Your father is right. It's time for us to let go and allow you to find out for yourselves what you want from life."

Alexis dived into Bethany Anne's arms, unable to bear seeing her mother caught between pride and the pain of parting. "I'm going to write and call every day if we can. I promise."

The elevator came to a stop, much to everybody's relief.

Michael exchanged wry glances with Bethany Anne as the door opened. "Consider this an adventure out of time," he told them as the door opened. "We'll be right here waiting for you."

They left the elevator and headed for where Trey was

waiting in the corridor. For all his six feet of wiry muscle, he still managed to broadcast his nervousness.

It was a sentiment shared by all four of them.

They followed in a half-daze while the adults talked and walked them through the vault to the Vid-doc chamber in the back.

Alexis inspected the equipment she was shown without taking any of it in. She would remember it all later, when her emotions had settled. At that moment, her mind was on what the next six years would hold for her and the others.

The goodbyes were over all too quickly, as was Eve's briefing before their immersion. All four could have been watching an episode of *Devon's Defenders* for all they retained of it.

Alexis blinked away sudden tears when it was time to get into the Vid-docs. She smiled when she felt K'aia's hand touch her shoulder.

K'aia nodded toward the Vid-doc shaped for her four-legged body. "See you in there."

Trey hugged his mother, taking in every detail of her face to make sure he didn't forget what she looked like. "I will make you proud, I swear it."

"I am already proud of you," Mahi' replied. Her voice was scratchy with emotion. "Be safe, my son."

Alexis swallowed her emotions and dashed between Bethany Anne and Michael for one last hug. "I'm going to miss you. I'll call as soon as we can."

Gabriel waited for Alexis to say goodbye to their father and mother before going to them. He met his mother's dark, sad eyes and found it impossible to say the actual word. He hugged Bethany Anne quickly. "See you in six years. Good luck on Qu'Baka."

K'aia waited for the others to say their farewells before shaking the adults' hands and wishing them luck with the battle ahead. "I'd better be going with you for the next one," she joked before climbing into her Vid-doc.

Bethany Anne spoke some final words of wisdom as they got settled on the neural mats.

"This is the first step of the rest of your lives. When I was young, people left home and had their coming of age out in the world. Some went to college, and others joined the military. Some found the path less traveled and got lost to find themselves. We can't give you that and keep you safe from our enemies. "

She blinked away tears as the Vid-doc lids closed on her children. "This is your world to claim. Make the most of it."

---

Bethany Anne's words echoed as their minds were transferred to the gameworld.

All at once, their avatars manifested, suspended in…

Nothing.

Alexis wrinkled her nose at the conclusion her senses came to. "Well, there can't just be *nothing*. There must be *something*."

Gabriel waved his hand in front of his face. "We're here. That's not 'nothing.'" He tried all the usual ways to interact with the gameworld. "Mom and Dad weren't kidding about us being on our own. I can't find any menus."

K'aia grunted in consternation. "There's no up or down! Your menus can wait. Where's the gravity?"

Trey growled in alarm at the way his fur floated up to stand on end. "Why isn't Eve here? She should be here, right?"

Gabriel was wondering the same thing. "Some light would be stellar, for a start."

The empty space beneath their feet became solid the same instant the space above them revealed its endless layers of sparkling stars.

The starlight spilled over a Salvadorian landscape, revealing the ground beneath the platforms they each stood on to be no more than a translucent two-dimensional line grid hovering on an improbable axis in the space between galaxies.

Alexis knelt to investigate what held their platforms a breath above the shimmering lines, then got to her feet, her curiosity piqued by finding nothing to connect any of their platforms to the extraordinary grid. "Don't move," she warned the others. "There's no saying we can't die here, and that looks like the kind of death you'd want to avoid." She glanced at the churning event horizon ringing the black hole at one end of the grid and shuddered.

*Very astute, Alexis,* Eve's voice came from all around them. *But the game has not yet begun, and you cannot die here.*

They froze on the spot, searching for the source of Eve's voice—and hopefully some guidance on beginning the program.

*Look up,* Eve told them not unkindly.

She laughed at the reaction when all four looked up and saw her smiling at them out of the stars.

Alexis forgot about the impossible physics; her attention was on the display in the inky darkness above. "Oh, my…"

"The stars," Trey breathed. "They look just like Eve!"

The twinkling points of light glowed increasingly brighter as they rearranged themselves and formed Eve's avatar.

Trey threw up an arm just before the starlight became too much for his unenhanced eyes to take.

The Eve-made-of-starlight dimmed a few million lumens as she glided gracefully from the heavens to float in front of the platforms.

K'aia threw a skeptical glare Eve's way. "Okay, what's going on? Why are we here?"

"Where *is* here?" Trey added. "It doesn't look anything like I expected."

Eve smiled serenely. "All in good time."

Alexis threw up a hand to indicate their surroundings. "Eve, you have to tell us something. Your briefing gave us barely anything to go on, except that we're supposed to have this realer-than-reality experience. Standing around on the Y-axis isn't exactly an everyday occurrence for me."

Gabriel nodded. "What Alexis said."

"Don't look at me," K'aia responded when Eve's amused gaze fell on her. "Point me at a threat I can comprehend, and I'm your Yollin. Otherwise, your bright young hopes are there." She jerked a thumb at the other platforms.

Trey lifted his hands. "I agree with Alexis. I don't see how this place has anything to do with the real-life experience you told us about in your briefing."

Eve lifted her hands and turned ninety degrees to indicate the black hole at the far edge of the grid. "You are currently in the rejuvenation cycle. There will be a few moments' wait while the neural nets are integrated. I created this space so your minds could remain conscious during the process."

Alexis noticed Trey's blank look. "She means while our brains are connected to the game system."

Trey nodded. "Oh. It's fun. Way better than being unconscious and waking up in a strange place. Thank you, Eve."

Eve inclined her head, and the four platforms rose an inch higher and tipped up at the back, startling all four into their ready stances. "It was a small effort, and the integration is improved by your minds being active. I hope you realize there's *always* room for fun."

Alexis saw the minute smirk on Eve's face and knew immediately that something big was coming. She crouched to keep her center of balance low and held her arms out to the sides.

The grid pulsed with light, then fell away in the center. The lines collapsed inward and stretched, forming a sheer drop that flicked up at the other end.

The lines glowed brighter as they settled, forming four distinct paths that rippled with synchronized light.

Gabriel whooped, almost falling off his platform when he worked out what was happening. "No way! It's a *ramp*!"

"Into the black hole?" K'aia couldn't believe the effort Eve had put into the loading room. "Eve, I forgive you for everything. This is amazing!"

Alexis pumped her fist without shifting her stance. "Way to go, Eve!"

Trey's cry of shock echoed around them. "You want to fire us into *that?*" He looked at the grins splitting his friends' faces, then settled into his ready stance. "Okay, if you're all happy with it."

Eve chuckled. "You will be fine, Tu'Reigd."

She lifted a hand, and the platforms were released simultaneously.

"Remember," Eve called as they hurtled down the breakneck incline, "life is what you make of it."

Gabriel's eyes widened as his platform picked up speed. He angled his body to meet the oncoming rush, a scream of joy escaping as his adrenaline hit heights that usually only came with the threat of impending death. "Last one through pays the forfeit!"

Alexis narrowed her eyes as Gabriel shot ahead. "Not. Happening." She increased her mass and leaned into the descent.

Trey dug in with his feet as the dip panned out. "I'm not getting stuck asking for a long weight again!" His platform wobbled as he shifted to keep it balanced. "It was two hours before the guys in requisitions gave in and told me it was a prank."

K'aia laughed as she overtook Alexis, then Gabriel. "No forfeit for me! I'm getting there first!"

Neck and neck, they crested the kick.

Their platforms stalled a moment when gravity crashed the party. The momentary disappointment was replaced by cheers when thrusters activated at the rear of each platform.

"Race!" Alexis yelled. She shot toward the event horizon with Gabriel on her heels, then Trey.

K'aia took an extra half-second to work out her thrusters. "Dammit! I'm *not* taking that forfeit!"

"Too late!" Alexis trilled. "I'm thro—"

Bright blue light filled their perception as Alexis crossed the threshold.

Gabriel was next.

K'aia cursed again when the blue light flashed for a third time, indicating Trey's progress into the game. "It had better not involve shoveling any kind of shit," she grumbled as the light swallowed her.

_____

## 2

### K'aia

Barien's body was heavy, and the sand was difficult to run on. At any moment, the guards would come pouring out of the salt mine, and then K'aia would be...

*Fine.*

K'aia stopped at the sound of Eve's voice. "I could kick myself." She didn't think she could be blamed for not realizing she was in a game scenario. The air tasted of salt, and she felt the weight of Barien's body pressing on the scar tissue across her shoulders. "Holy hellfire, this is beyond real. I'm living it all over again."

She paused to place Barien gently under the tree. It didn't matter to her that this was a construct. It didn't *feel* like one. This human had been her friend.

"I get to say goodbye again," she murmured as she covered the tapestry she'd wrapped him in with leafy branches. "Who gets that chance? I wish you could have made it. You would have loved living with the Empress and her family."

K'aia got to her four feet and looked around. "So, I'm on Devon. Well, Belv'th at this point in history."

Eve declined to reply.

That wasn't a problem. K'aia knew her own memory. She'd escaped from the mine near City-on-the-Lakes. "Where are Bethany Anne and Michael?"

No reply again. They should be here somewhere to kick off the revenge portion of this memory. If they weren't here already...

"They're not coming."

The guards would be here any second. She had to keep running.

K'aia checked herself again. "Do I? Do I *have* to run? I'm not a slave, helpless to take my own vengeance. I'm a grown-ass Yollin who has trained to be better than any mercenary on this shithole planet."

She broke a thick branch off the tree and marched over to where the guards were gathering.

K'aia lifted her chin and readied the branch to face her demons. "Just watch."

*Try this,* Eve whispered into K'aia's mind.

The branch became a worked-metal staff with a red gem on one end that glowed with Etheric energy.

K'aia grinned at the unexpected gift. "A Baka staff? Well, thanks."

Eve's chuckle echoed as her voice faded. *Pass it on to Trey when you meet.*

K'aia plowed into the forty and more guards who were eyeing her like she was a fine cut of steak and they'd been fasting for a month. *You've got it. It might be a bit dinged up from some of these hard heads.*

The guards were just as dense as K'aia remembered from the real encounter.

They went down a lot easier this time around, although K'aia wasn't sure how much of that was her enhancement and training, and how much was the game limiting the abilities of the NPCs. The game-generated characters Eve had built from her memory were exquisitely detailed, as was the scene—from the taste of salt on the air down to the last dumbass comment from the guards.

K'aia decided it was her awesomeness that was the differing factor. After all her time training with Addix and Tabitha, this was playing out like the dreams she'd had when she first escaped the mines. Therapeutic benefits of the scenario aside, she had to start the game for real.

She skipped chatting with the mine boss and went straight for his stupid face with the explode-y end of the Baka staff.

With him out of the way, the remainder of the guards ran.

K'aia was disappointed the fight had been so quick, but she had other things on her mind. Namely, finding the twins.

It wasn't sitting well that they were separated. This was the longest she had let them out of her sight since the stunt they'd pulled with the *Izanami*.

Legendary, no doubt. But had they taken their guard? No.

K'aia wasn't feeling any happier that they were confined to the gameworld.

Although, how much trouble could they get into? She

supposed she had little to complain about. The worst that could happen here was, they got reset a few times.

As a guard, it could be much, much harder. She'd shadowed John one time during her bodyguard training when Addix was away. The stories she'd heard from him about Bethany Anne were enough to put a Yollin into an early grave.

K'aia shook off her rambling thoughts and sat on a rock to clean the NPC blood off the end of the staff and consider her next move. The logical thing was to make her way to First City, where she could pick up Trey and wait for Alexis and Gabriel to get here.

It was on the twins to find her if they were elsewhere in the galaxy. They would have access to a spaceship—or they would give themselves access to one, more likely—and they would make their way here to Belv'th.

The name was weird to her. Alien, her mind supplied with a snicker. "I'm calling this place Devon whether it is or not. Maybe we'll make it into Devon. Now, where's that skinny-ass Baka?"

### Trey

Trey knew he was inside the game to learn grace under pressure, as well as to train and make the most of the enhancements Bethany Anne had gifted him.

However, Ch'Irzt's jealousy had marred every day of Trey's life, and the gameworld was just as they'd been promised. This was realer-than-real, and his cousin was at his *most* punchable.

What else was he to do when presented with this gift-wrapped opportunity for catharsis?

"Screw *you!*" Trey landed a hard right on Ch'Irzt's jaw. From the moment he'd gotten into the game, his cousin had been begging for a beating. "I'm done listening to your dumb ass talk crap."

Ch'Irzt landed on his backside with a satisfying thud. He glared sullenly at Trey, raising his fists as he got to his feet. "Oh, now you've gone and done it," he threatened. "Just wait. I'm going to beat your scrawny ass all over the palace, and *then* I'm going to hand you to my father for your real punishment."

Trey blocked Ch'Irzt's attack and knocked him back with a well-placed foot to the abdomen. "I don't care if Da'Mahin thinks he's the emperor of the freaking universe. He can't tell me a thing. Where is my mother?"

Da'Mahin walked in as his son landed roughly on the floor for a second time. He rounded on Tu'Reigd with an angry growl. "*You* are banished, and still I keep finding you here. Get *out*, and be thankful I am merciful on behalf of my sister. I should have you whipped for not knowing your place."

Trey lunged at his uncle. "Try it." He smirked, pleased by Da'Mahin's minute flinch. "Remember, my place was stolen by *you.* Your day is coming, Uncle."

He stormed past Da'Mahin and out into the streets of First City. The sky was the wrong color; it was too bright. Where was the QBBS *Guardian?* He couldn't see it up there.

"Maybe I made a mistake?" Trey murmured as the aggression drained out of him, leaving behind the realization that he had no idea where to go. Everything that made life good was gone. Was this the next six years of his existence? Trapped on a world where everything was out of place?

Trey panicked. He crossed the bazaar in a blind rush, only slowing when he found a cattle market where Hexagon Plaza should have been.

He wandered aimlessly toward the market, his mind refusing to process his surroundings. Neither could he grasp the depth of the difference one person made to his happiness in life.

Where was Bethany Anne?

*Open your eyes.*

Trey's eyes shot open at the sound of Eve's voice inside his mind. He dropped to the ground just before he was knocked down by a cattle trailer speeding into the market.

Hot air blew into his face as the hovercraft passed over him. Trey rolled to the side of the road and got to his feet.

He dusted himself off, taking measured breaths to get his heart rate under control. The last thing he needed was an early death and a restart back at the Enclave.

Mahi' would know what to do. His Mahi' wasn't here, though. Trey had decided on arrival that it would be too painful to try to interact with the Mahi' construct in the gameworld.

He looked up at the sky and howled curses, uncaring of the looks he drew from passersby. "This game sucks, Eve! This *planet* sucks! Where are Gabriel and Alexis and K'aia? Where is *everything*?"

Eve spoke into his mind. *In this reality, Bethany Anne chose another planet to visit.*

Trey froze to the spot. *This is what would have happened without her?*

*Yes,* Eve replied. *This is still Belv'th. Devon was never founded.*

*No Bethany Anne?* Trey didn't comprehend Eve's words. His mind was on his gratitude that this wasn't his reality.

But it was. For the next six years.

A crushing thought occurred to him as the news sank in. "What else is different? Are Gabriel and Alexis even on this planet?"

*Not at present.*

Trey's heart sank further. "It's going to take them a while to get here. Huh. What about K'aia?"

*You can find her if you know where to look.*

Trey didn't have a clue. "How can I possibly know where she is? She could be anywhere on the planet if she didn't meet Bethany Anne and Michael."

He thought about what K'aia had told him of her quest to join up with Bethany Anne. "But I know K'aia. She would find somewhere she could lie low and earn a living from fighting. What I need is to find a map. This is not the city I know."

*Ask, and you shall receive,* Eve replied.

Trey grinned at the holo that appeared on his left wrist. Eve might be a PITA with her mysterious answers, but she always came through when she was needed.

He tapped his holo to activate it. "It's a start. Can I get the Empress here now?"

*Nice try, Tu'Reigd,* Eve chuckled. *No cookie. Now, turn around.*

.  .  .

**Alexis and Gabriel**

Gabriel nudged Alexis with his mind. *It* looks *like Mom.*

*Sounds like her, too,* Alexis agreed.

They continued to listen intently to the conversation in the throne room from the doorway to the right of the dais.

Alexis wrinkled her nose. *But something is off.*

*There's no imitating Mom,* Gabriel decided, feeling the same spark missing from the NPC. *Eve did a really good job, but it's not fooling me. It's like...we can predict what this Mom would do. Nobody knows what Mom would really do.*

Alexis understood what her brother meant, even if he didn't. *You can't program true randomness, just like you can't catch a hurricane in a jar. Mom is her own force, so she can't be predicted.*

There was a break in the monotony of requests for trade agreements, border disputes, and various politicians acting on behalf of independent governments when Michael left Bethany Anne's side to remove a reptilian alien from the line.

Bethany Anne watched disinterestedly while Michael and John escorted the ill-intentioned ambassador from the throne room.

*Her joy,* Gabriel concluded. *That's what's missing. Mom always says how much she hated being Empress.*

*Not so much the Empressing part,* Alexis countered with a wave of her hand that mirrored Bethany Anne's. *Just, well, this.*

Gabriel eyed the never-ending line of people waiting for an audience with Bethany Anne. *"This" is a large part of leadership. Do you think you'll be okay with being responsible for whole worlds?*

Alexis frowned while she gave the question its full consideration. *I don't mind the ones who come here in genuine need of our help, but they're not the only ones asking for Mom's time. We wouldn't be able to do it alone.*

Gabriel made a small sound of agreement. *Mom has Dad and our uncles and aunts to protect her, along with ADAM and TOM. We would be alone unless we had friends and family we could rely on the same way.*

Alexis smiled, warmed to the bones by the thought of their friends. *We have people we can rely on to have our backs, like K'aia and Trey.*

Gabriel nodded his agreement. *Like K'aia and Trey.*

Alexis pressed her lips together. *Do you miss Phyrro?*

Gabriel chuckled at the memory of their EI tutor from childhood. *Yeah, but I don't miss his lessons. What made you think of Phyrro?*

Alexis shrugged. *I don't know. I was thinking about Mom having ADAM to take care of everything she has to hold in her mind.*

Gabriel was done watching the action in the throne room. *We should get moving. If we're in an alternative universe, then they're both on whatever Devon was called before Mom took it over.*

Alexis grabbed Gabriel before he could go. *Wait, I see Eve.*

*You think that's our Eve?* Gabriel asked. *Why would she create all these NPCs and play herself?*

Alexis decided that bit of womanly wisdom was best kept to herself. *Why not?*

Eve fixed the twins with a smile.

Gabriel furrowed his brow. *No way. How did you know?*

*Oh, lucky guess,* Alexis returned Eve's smile with an enthusiastic wave. *Let's see what we can get her to tell us.*

Eve glided purposefully through a door at the opposite end of the room. The twins followed, being careful not to get caught up in the line for the throne.

They found her waiting for them in the antechamber beyond. She smiled at Alexis and Gabriel, spreading her hands as wide as her grin. "Are you impressed?"

"Completely," Alexis enthused. "You rebuilt the whole universe inside a game. I take it we are on the *Meredith Reynolds?*"

"Your twist is that the Federation was never formed," Gabriel mused. "We get it. What does that mean for K'aia and Trey?"

"What does it mean for Devon?" Alexis expanded, her voice rising with the sheer scale of the changes to everything they'd always taken as a given. "What about the Interdiction? Who is there to prevent the Seven from tearing through and killing everyone?"

Eve manifested her usual composure, meeting their questions with her serene smile. "It means Devon doesn't exist, and that the Seven don't dare come within scanner distance of anywhere the Empress decrees is hers to protect. The game began at the moment in time your parents would have altered Belv'th's path."

Alexis gasped, the extent of the gameworld becoming clear to her. "That's… Eve, how long did this take to build?"

Gabriel sighed at his sister's innate ability to be distracted by every bit of shiny technology that came along. "Stay focused, Alexis. We need to get to Bel…whatever it's called in this reality. What happens if one of Trey's uncles kills him before we get there? Do we all reset?"

Eve shook her head. "No, you will reset to the moment before you died. There were some concessions that had to be made for your starting positions. Once you are together, any death will trigger a group reset to the beginning of the last objective chain." She looked into the distance. "I advise you get to the *Gemini* sooner rather than later."

The twins gave Eve identical confused looks.

"The *Gemini*?" Alexis asked.

"How do we find an objective chain?" Gabriel cut in.

Eve tilted her head toward them, the smile in her eyes missing the spark of life from a moment ago. "Hello, children. Is there something I can help you with?"

*Too late,* Gabriel groaned, realizing immediately that the real Eve had departed the NPC avatar. *She's gone.*

Alexis grabbed Gabriel's hand and pulled him out of the anteroom. *She gave us the name of a ship. We've just got to find out where it is.*


### Belv'th, First City

K'aia couldn't believe the difference between the city she knew and the one she was in.

The streets thrummed with a low, angry energy that was entirely absent on Devon. She knew the unspoken words by heart. The language of oppression didn't change from setting to setting.

She was drawing attention. People were pointing and whispering snide remarks about her being far from home.

One thing that was exactly the same was the scarcity of four-legged Yollins in her locale.

This planet just wasn't appealing to anyone who could live by legitimate means on Yoll. K'aia had long suspected her family operated on the shady side of things when it came to earning a living. This time around, she hadn't visited the wreck of their old house, not wanting to find proof of her suspicions with wiser eyes.

Maybe she *should* have gone searching for the truth. It wouldn't have been worse than what she was seeing here in the city. Without fear of reprisal from Baba Yaga, the slave trade was in full swing in the market squares, as were the fights.

K'aia had mostly forgotten how First City had been a stew with a fetid mixture of pirates, mercenaries, and asshole bullies before Bethany Anne had laid down the law. It didn't matter who held the money. They were all bent on forcing ordinary people who found themselves in hard places into even worse situations.

Like the fighters in the shabby ring in front of her. K'aia knew desperation when she saw it. One of the two would kill the other for the sake of a handful of credits to feed their family, and K'aia was angered by it. There was no judgment to be passed on the fighters, only pity for them, and whichever family would be short a provider, come the end of the fight.

The responsibility was with the fight-runners. K'aia's list of things they ought to do something about was growing longer by the minute, but there wasn't a whole lot she could accomplish by herself.

Which meant she should stop wasting time pining for a

planet that wasn't real and find the one person on it who was.

Easier said than done.

K'aia picked up her pace. She skirted the bazaar, knowing she would be slowed to the point of frustration by the mid-afternoon crowd.

Nothing would be simpler than strolling over to the Enclave and finding him there, but she knew Trey. He wouldn't have stayed where he had entered the gameworld.

K'aia's hunch was rewarded by the sight of Trey's golden fur a few hundred feet away in what should have been Hexagon Plaza. He was standing in the middle of the road, shouting curses at the sky. "Kid's going to get himself killed."

She started forward when she spotted the speeding cattle truck; her prediction looked like it was about to become a reality. There was no way she was going to reach him in time. Her heart lurched in her chest as the plea tumbled from her mouth. "Eve, please don't let that dumbass die just yet?"

Trey dropped flat to the ground in the instant before the trailer thundered over him.

"If that was you, thank you." K'aia breathed a sigh of relief and resumed her progress toward Trey's position. The crowds sucked, but then, crowds did when you were the size of a small vehicle and weren't the most graceful around the rear end.

The staff Eve had given her helped. A few pokes with the inactive end cleared the more obstinate shoppers quickly enough.

Trey got to his feet as K'aia approached, the storm of

emotion passing from his expression at the sight of her. "K'aia! Eve had me thinking I had to search the whole city for you."

K'aia passed Trey the staff, snickering at his look of surprise at being handed what was still prototype technology. "Eve is an ass. She makes up for it in other ways."

Trey's eyes widened at K'aia's daring. "Eve is a delight. I won't hear any different. Look at this!" He brandished the staff. "I could teach Da'Mahin a thing or two with this if that mangy asshole was worth my time."

K'aia snorted her laughter. "Yeah, sure. C'mon, we need to find a place to set up a base of operations for when the twins get here. I'm guessing we're not going to get a warm welcome in the Enclave."

A slow grin spread over Trey's face. His horizon had grown infinitely brighter now that he wasn't facing it alone. "I don't know, a lashing gets you pretty warmed up, right?" He couldn't hold his laughter in for long. "This isn't so bad. I've got an idea or two about where we can find a base. What are you thinking for size?"

K'aia's chest heaved as she struggled to control her laughter. "I don't know. We'll need room for whatever ship the twins manage to get their hands on."

Trey set off for the bazaar at a jog, slipping through the crowd easily. "Follow me. I know the perfect place."

K'aia shouldered her way through the shoppers after Trey. "As long as it's perfect and cheap. We're not exactly rolling in credits."

Trey paused to wait for K'aia to catch up. "This is a game. I had no problem relieving Ch'Irzt of the contents of his pockets." He flipped a credit chip and caught it in his hand, then passed it to K'aia. "You should probably keep that. You know I'll lose it."

K'aia examined the chip before shucking off her pack and stowing it safely inside. "Fifty thousand is a good start. We're going to need plenty more than that, though."

Trey shrugged. "We can get fat on the proceeds of crime." He grinned at K'aia's look of disdain. "Not like that. Wanna go shut down some illegal fights?"

K'aia punched Trey in the arm and moved to get ahead of him in the crowd. "Why didn't you say so? I know just where to start."

## 3

**Heart of the Empire, QBBS *Meredith Reynolds***

Alexis, who was fiddling with a panel she was using to hack Meredith, paused. *Are we clear?*

Gabriel scanned the area quickly and ducked back around the corner. *Yeah, it was a civilian. Are you having any success with persuading Meredith to reveal the location of the ship?*

Alexis was surprised by Gabriel's surge of frustration. *I'm getting there. It doesn't feel right to mess with her, so I'm sneaking around disguised as a routine system inquiry. You okay?* She continued her search of the system for any mention of the *Gemini* project.

Gabriel nodded without turning from his lookout position. *Yeah. The game isn't what I expected, is all. This is exactly the same situation we were in with the* Izanami.

*You couldn't have expected this, surely?* Alexis debated how anyone could be prepared for the total immersion. *Eve created a ton of scenarios, but they all had a narrative we had to follow. We are the narrators in this universe. The question is, what are our parents expecting of us?*

*Double dammit.* Gabriel left his place and picked up the small toolbox Alexis was using. *We haven't learned our lesson at all. We aren't going to find the ship in the system.*

Alexis groaned. *You're right. Mom wouldn't put something meant for us where just anyone could find it. We have to ask permission to leave, don't we?*

Gabriel nodded and handed her the toolbox. *Think of it as an inoculation. We have to leave home for real at some point, right? We'll get to gauge how badly Mom's going to blow her top when it happens.*

Alexis snickered. *Maybe I should introduce a boyfriend to Dad while we're here?*

*You have a boyfriend?* Gabriel's disposition darkened instantly at the thought of any male near his sister. *Why haven't I met him?*

Alexis fixed Gabriel with an icy stare. *Rein in your caveman attitude. I was joking, and you are just as bad as Dad.* She flounced off to find their gameworld parents, thoroughly annoyed with her brother.

Gabriel, for his part, had no clue what he'd done. He hurried to fall into step beside her. *Sorry? I don't know why, but please accept my apology before we miss something vital to getting the best outcome.*

Alexis sighed. She wasn't being fair. *It's starting to sink in that we're here instead of home. It's going to be a challenge to keep ourselves from getting so deep into this world that we forget what's real and what's not. I shouldn't take it out on you.*

Gabriel bumped her arm with his elbow. *What are*

*brothers for? We're both feeling out of place, so it's only natural. All we have to do is be good to each other, and we'll get through it just fine.*

Alexis felt her confidence return. *You're right. Our friends will be wondering where we are. We have to focus on getting to them, so whatever comes next can wait.*

They found Bethany Anne alone in her private quarters.

Bethany Anne looked up and smiled when Gabriel and Alexis popped their heads around the door. "I was wondering how long it would be before you two got here. Come in."

Alexis felt Gabriel's discomfort with the NPC. She smiled and went over to give Bethany Anne a hug like she normally did when she saw her mother. "Hi, Mom."

Gabriel stood back to give Alexis room to take the lead.

Bethany Anne's knowing smile was just the same as it had been every day of their lives. "Why do you both have that 'I want' look? Sit down and let's talk."

Alexis took the seat beside Bethany Anne at her writing desk and waited for Gabriel to perch on the arm of the loveseat behind her before beginning. "It's not something we want. It's something we need. We came to ask for your permission to leave the *Meredith Reynolds* and explore beyond the Empire."

She closed her eyes and waited for the inevitable explosion and scene switch. However, they did not find themselves in an underground bunker at a wave of Bethany Anne's hand.

Gabriel looked at Bethany Anne in total confusion. This

wasn't the reaction either of them had been expecting. "You're smiling. Why are you smiling?"

Bethany Anne stood up and headed straight for the door. "Your father and I saw this coming a while ago. Come with me."

Gabriel wiggled his eyebrows at Alexis as he got up to follow Bethany Anne. *What do you know? It wasn't so sucky after all.*

Alexis stuck out a foot to trip him. You *suck. You get to tell her the next time.*

Gabriel evaded the trap easily. *Nice try, sis.* He smirked at Alexis and slipped out into the corridor.

"Where are we going?" Alexis asked as she and Gabriel fell into step on either side of Bethany Anne.

"To my hangar," Bethany Anne told them without slowing her pace. "You aren't going anywhere without my full protection."

Alexis narrowed her eyes playfully. "You're just letting us go? No fight? Who are you, and what have you done with our mom?"

Bethany Anne chuckled. "I won the bet on whether you two would ask permission before leaving, so I'm happy. Besides, you're growing up, and it's only rational you would want to stretch your legs and see some of the universe."

*Mom had something to do with this,* Gabriel stated conclusively. *Our real mom, I mean. Dad, too. This was a test, I know it.*

Alexis nodded. *I think so, too. But we passed, which means we get all the good toys to play with. I'm glad we worked it out. Mom loves to go overboard, whether she'll admit it or not.*

Her words dried up in her mouth when they entered Bethany Anne's hangar.

"Welcome to the QGE *Gemini*." Bethany Anne swept her arms wide to indicate the shining blue ship. "What do you think of your ride?"

Alexis stopped in her tracks, a squeal sneaking out despite herself when she saw the modulated design of the ship. "She's *beautiful*! So different from the warships we're used to." She darted across the hangar to get a look at the name stenciled on the curved flank, swerving to account for the outward-canted legs. "QGE? What class of ship is she?"

Bethany Anne led the twins underneath the ship. "The *Gemini* is a galactic explorer-class starship. Your EI will instruct you on its capabilities once you're aboard."

Her face softened as she came to a stop beneath the larger of two hatches in the belly of the ship. "Your father and I have stocked the holds with everything we thought you might need for an expedition. Be brave, my loves. Remember who you are and what you stand for."

*Look at her face,* Gabriel murmured. *This is a recording of Mom. Do you think anyone can inhabit their avatar?*

Alexis threw herself into Bethany Anne's arms, over-come with the same mixed emotions she felt coming from her brother. *This is going to be very hard to bear if the game keeps crossing with reality.*

Even Gabriel got his hug this time. He found embracing the avatar uncomfortable, but it was his last chance to feel his mother's love for a while. "Bye, Mom. We'll make you and Dad proud. Promise."

The hatch slid out and across, and a ramp wide enough

for a roamer descended to meet them. Gabriel's eyes grew wide at the female silhouette standing inside the hatch. "That doesn't look like Izanami."

Bethany Anne chuckled. "Well, this is your ship, made for you. You take care of Gemini, and she will take care of you." She shooed Gabriel and Alexis onto the ramp, her eyes misty. "I'll leave you three to get acquainted. Make sure you call home once in a while, okay?"

"We will," they promised as Bethany Anne moved out of the shadow of the ship.

Side by side, Alexis and Gabriel walked up the ramp and boarded the *Gemini* for the first time.

Lights came on overhead when they entered the cargo bay in the rear module of the ship. The first thing they saw was the double line of vehicles in the center of the cargo bay. The next was the owner of the silhouette, a smooth-faced EI with features somewhere between Baba Yaga's and Eve's.

Gabriel smiled and introduced himself. "But you already know who we are, right?"

The EI glided toward Gabriel and Alexis, the intermittent static in her avatar marking it as a holoprojection. "I am Gemini, and yes, I know who you are. Welcome aboard, Captains. If you would follow me, we will take a tour of the ship before we depart."

Alexis narrowed her eyes. "Captains? Ships usually have one captain."

Gemini glided slightly ahead, her footsteps falling a hair's breadth above the carpeted floor. "This ship can be called many things, but 'usual' is not one of them. "

Gabriel frowned, the corner of his mouth turning up in bemusement. *Alexis, I think she might be real.*

Alexis also recognized the hallmarks of an unrestricted personality matrix in the EI. *Maybe. It could be that one of the objective chains Eve hinted at is helping Gemini ascend to AI status.*

Gemini turned her body to face the twins without pausing in her steady progression. "If you are ready, we have a lot to cover before we leave." She smiled at Alexis' and Gabriel's indications to continue. "The *Gemini* is a galactic explorer-class starship. We are equipped with the latest in navigation, shields, cloaking, and weapons."

Alexis accessed the ship's systems in her HUD and pulled up their offensive capabilities. "We can convert Etheric energy into weaponized plasma? That's going to come in handy."

Gabriel was similarly impressed with what he found in the defenses. "The outer shields can be converted to emit an EMP pulse. We're protected by the inner layer."

Gemini followed the back and forth with growing concern. "I am confused. My directives tell me that our mission is to explore. We are to act as diplomats and ambassadors for the Etheric Empire. We do not need to compound the popular myth that all humans are aggressive and deadly. It is to be hoped that we will avoid confrontation whenever possible."

Alexis nodded solemnly, understanding Gemini's reticence. "It's our hope, too. Unfortunately, we know to expect differently. Our expedition won't consist entirely of peaceful encounters. There are a lot of isolated planets and strange new worlds to explore once we leave the Empire. The systems beyond the borders can be feral, rife with dangerous people and organizations that have no regard for justice or freedom."

"We don't want to give the wrong impression, either," Gabriel clarified. "Humans *are* aggressive and deadly—when it's necessary. We were not raised to allow evil to prevail when we have the power to prevent it."

"That's true," Alexis told Gemini firmly. "Wanting to live in peace is great when everyone else wants the same thing, but standing by while bad things happen would make us no better than the ones committing the evil."

Gemini's avatar flickered while she devoted extra cycles to the contradictory statement. "You are saying that to prevent violence, you must commit violence? I fail to understand the logic."

Gabriel lifted his hands. "I agree, but what can you do? We don't make the rules. We just have to use them to our advantage, same as everyone else."

Alexis smirked. "Only *we* play to win. Our mom always says the only fair fight is one you lose."

Gemini absorbed the information with interest. "I will consider the varying consequences of unplanned contact with new species."

Gemini's tour began with an elevator ride that let out on the mezzanine level of the bridge. "This is the navigation center. The lower-level access opens onto your ready room, where the long-distance communications are placed."

Gabriel took the stairs three at a time and made a

beeline for the twin captain's chairs set head-on to the curved viewscreen and the console beneath. "Which side do you want?"

Alexis inspected the two stations before settling on the right-hand chair. "This one."

"I'm going to check out the ready room."

Gemini crossed paths with Gabriel as she came to stand by Alexis with her hands on her hips. "We should continue with the tour. We still have engineering, the armory, the forward cargo hold, your personal quarters—"

Alexis activated the heads-up display built into her chair's headrest. "We have all the time in the world for that. We need to locate a planet by the name of Belv'th and get there as quickly as the ship can take us."

Gemini gave Alexis a pointed look. "You would have been learning how fast the ship can travel right now if you had not abandoned the introduction tour."

"Okay," Alexis held back the command in her tone for the sake of teaching the new EI how to work with them. "However, a request from one of us has priority over anything nonessential in your queue. This is how we handle a conflict of interest. Put in the request for departure with Meredith. We will continue the tour once we are underway."

Gemini paused to process the change to her secondary directives and send the request to the station's EI. She received the go-ahead in the next instant. "Very well. We are clear to depart."

"Thank you, Gemini." Alexis smiled and went back to inputting Devon's coordinates into the navigation interface from memory. She had an inkling that the reason so many AIs had borderline personality issues—and not so borderline in some cases—was that humans in stressful situations reached for anger or humor before any other response. "Set a course for these coordinates and take us out."

She intended to deal differently with Gemini. Time would tell if a more nurturing approach made a difference.

### Belv'th, First City (three weeks later)

Trey eyed the wall of armed muscle around the Noel-ni taking bets on the fight inside the ring. "More security than the last one. They're getting nervous."

"Haven't you heard?" K'aia murmured amusedly. "There's a pair of vigilantes in the city. It's not safe for anyone trying to do a dishonest day's work anymore."

Trey snickered. "I heard. Rumor has it they're undefeatable." He adjusted his mask where it had slipped down, then pointed his staff at a corner support of the ring and fired. "Especially the two-legged one. Watch this."

Trey chose his target and fired another charge the moment the ring collapsed.

The water tower on the opposite side of the square exploded, causing panic. People stampeded to get out of the way of the flash flood, diverting the attention of the guards from their duty.

Trey relaxed his stance. "All yours," he told K'aia with a grin.

K'aia shot him a disgruntled look and headed into the chaos he'd created.

Trey stood back to watch, wishing he had the ability to move like the wind already. Freed from the need to hide her abilities by the disguise she wore, K'aia moved faster than he could clearly see. He just about made out the blur of her where the crowd parted.

The fight-runner's guards had been scattered by the flood. They recovered too slowly to save their boss from the Yollin who barreled in at super speed.

K'aia took down the Noel-ni with a swift kick to the throat.

He dropped to his knees, clutching his throat with fat hands covered in jeweled rings.

K'aia saw what she'd come for. She snatched the credit chip off the chain around his neck while he struggled to regain his breath and was back at Trey's side in a flash.

She dangled the chip in front of Trey before stashing it in a pouch on her belt. "All ours, you mean. That guy had *rubies* set into his canines, can you believe that? This should have a good amount on it. Maybe we can afford that food-printing unit we saw."

Trey pointed behind K'aia. "All we have to do is survive long enough to go buy it ."

K'aia turned the top of her body and saw that the Noel-ni's guards had recovered and were headed their way. "They look a bit annoyed. Wanna get out of here?"

Trey laughed as he and K'aia dashed away from the chaos in the square. He turned as he ran and waved at their angry pursuers. "Tell your boss we'd stick around, but his event was a total washout."

K'aia snorted and grabbed Trey's sleeve to turn him

around. "Quit clowning around and look for an escape route before they catch us!"

They pounded through the sandstone streets in silence, their attention on keeping track of the guards behind them. K'aia's enhancement and Trey's natural running pace was enough to put some distance between them and a messy ending on the pointy ends of the guards' swords.

K'aia pulled Trey into a dead-end alley off the side street they were on without slowing. "We need a place to hide," she panted. "They're not getting bored."

Trey sucked heaving breaths in until the hot bands crushing his lungs eased off a little. He lifted his head once the constriction in his chest began to fade and spotted the ladder protruding from the side of a building at the other end of the street. "What about that?"

K'aia saw the fire escape at the same time as Trey. "Race you."

Trey didn't have the wind to whine about her apparently endless energy. He forced his cramped leg muscles to pump out a few more steps to get him to the ladder and paused to rest his hands on his knees. "You go first. I need a minute still."

K'aia picked up angry voices nearby. "We haven't got a minute, unless you want to reset and lose the loot?" She leapt for the outside of the ladder and pulled herself up a few rungs, then gripped with her back legs and swung her upper body down to grab Trey's hands as she'd learned in training. "C'mon, I can't hold this all day like Addix can."

Trey grasped K'aia's hands and tried not to whoop as she swung him above her. He let go, grabbed the ladder, and pushed himself to climb the fire escape as fast as his adrenaline-filled body would carry him.

K'aia followed, pausing at the switchback halfway to pull up the bottom ladder and hide their route.

They heaved themselves over the lip of the roof one at a time and collapsed against the cool stone just moments before the street below was filled with the echoes of rough voices.

# 4

Trey peered over the edge to see what was going on below. He wished once again that he had a clue of how to activate his enhancements so he could do more than cower on a rooftop. A shortcut into the Etheric would be handy right about now.

Unfortunately, the result was the same as the last time he'd hoped for it to happen, and the time before that. "There are more people down there, not just that Noel-ni's guards."

K'aia glanced at the nearby buildings as the voices below grew louder. The roof sloped up from the ledge they were using for cover, flattening out twenty feet away before dropping off without any boundary to prevent a running jump. "That looks promising."

She made her way over to the other edge, her heart sinking when she saw the distance and the drop to the spiky roof of the next building over. Trey couldn't survive that, and even she would be pressed to land without breaking her legs.

K'aia edged back to Trey's position. "There's no way off this roof. Maybe we should fight them off. Are they all armed?"

Trey glanced at K'aia and nodded. "Yeah. It looks like half the criminals in the city decided to get in on the chase." He waved her over. "You need to see this before we decide anything. I think that's the Shrillexian we shut down last week."

"What are they doing?" K'aia stayed low as she crept over to join Trey. She scanned the mob, also recognizing a few familiar faces from their exploits during the last few weeks. "Yeah, that's him. We'll have to wait them out.""

Trey ducked away from the edge and sat with his back against the ledge. "You sure? They're going to figure out we're up here soon enough."

K'aia couldn't see an immediate way out of their predicament. "You're not wrong, but there's nowhere for us to go. It's too far for you to jump to another roof." She settled herself next to Trey and retrieved the credit chip from the pouch she'd secreted it in earlier. "We should see if it's even worth all this trouble."

Trey held out his hand for the chip. He swiped it against his wrist-holo, his eyes bugging out at the line of zeroes that flashed up on the display. He transferred the balance to their holding account. "Um, yeah. We don't want to lose this if we can help it."

K'aia sucked in a breath when Trey angled his wrist to show her the account they held all of the takings from their anti-crime spree in. "We could fund our own Hexagon with a few more shakedowns like that."

Trey grinned. "You want a media empire?"

K'aia grimaced. "No way. I'd be happy with a secure base we can work from and a way off the planet that doesn't involve us having to appropriate the ill-gotten wealth of every scumbag in the city to pay for it."

Trey nodded. "I'd settle for a place to train in peace. I'm here to prepare for leadership. I can't see how vigilantism is doing that."

K'aia shrugged. "You're gaining some experience of what it's like to live with nothing. We've been here less than a month. Give it time." She held up a hand, hearing the ladder rattle. "Crapsticks. We're out of time."

Trey risked a glance at the ladder. "Our Shrillexian friend. I have an idea." He grabbed the staff from his back and leaned over the edge.

"What are you doing?" K'aia hissed. "They'll see you!"

Trey activated the staff and fired at the bolts fixing the ladder to the wall. "Yeah, but they won't be able to get to us." He blasted the next set of bolts lower down and the fire escape peeled away from the wall, taking the Shrillexian with it.

He wiggled his fingers at the Shrillexian.

The falling Shrillexian screamed curses at Trey right up until the moment his head bounced off the ground. The ladder landed on top of him and the two nearest criminals.

The rest must have put their minds together and come up with a functioning brain cell to share. They looked up at the fading glow from Trey's staff and scattered to find a way into the building.

Trey looked at his inert staff with dismay. "I hope this thing has a way to recharge."

"Eve didn't say." K'aia indicated Trey climb onto her

back after a jerk of her head. "Get on. We have to risk the jump."

Trey was reluctant to take her up on the offer. He readied himself for the run-up and set off sprinting toward the flat end of the roof.

K'aia raced after him. "Trey, no!"

Too late; Trey made the leap. He realized he had no landing only after his feet had left the relative safety of the rooftop.

K'aia was helpless to act. She saw the moment Trey worked out he wasn't going to make it. "Dammit! We have to do all of this again, Trey! Did no one ever teach you to look before you leap?"

Trey heard K'aia distantly. This was it, his first-ever death inside the gameworld. The spikes on the roof below rushed up to meet his body, or the other way around, Trey wasn't sure. Either way, the two were going to meet any second.

He opened his eyes when the expected impalement failed to occur. He was jerked upward by some invisible force that cradled his entire body, stopping just inches away from becoming a Baka kebab.

There was a familiar giggle somewhere above Trey. He craned his neck to see Gabriel and Alexis peering out of a rectangular hole in the sky high above both buildings.

Gabriel nodded stoically. "Need a ride?"

Alexis moved her hands, and Trey rose slowly into the air and floated toward K'aia.

He grinned, keeping very still until his feet were safely on the roof in case Alexis dropped him. "You have no idea how glad I am to see you two."

Alexis giggled again. "Um, yeah, I think I do."

K'aia snorted and punched him in the arm. "Don't you ever do that again!"

Trey rubbed his arm, still grinning with the relief of avoiding death. "I'll try not to."

"Wait there," Gabriel told K'aia and Trey. "We'll send down a Pod."

## QGE *Gemini*, Galley

Trey focused on his food while K'aia told the story of their time in First City.

Alexis held up a hand and gave K'aia a high-five. "That explains how you managed to buy the property we're headed for when you started the game with nothing."

"Resourceful," Gabriel told her with a smile. "You guys did well."

K'aia grinned, her carapace pinkening with pride—and relief that the twins were here at last. "All we had to do was remember all the places Sabine's group visited after the initial smackdown Bethany Anne put on this cesspit in the real world. We've taken all of that wealth out of the criminals' hands and put it aside for when you two got here. The only concession we made was the base since it was too good a deal to pass up."

"Nice!" Gabriel shook with laughter as K'aia demonstrated the final heist with the various items on the table.

K'aia pushed the condiments and cups out of the way and directed her attention to the pizza. "You should have seen his face. I love teaching empathy to assholes. There's this look they always get, like they're not sure how they ended up on that side of the beating."

Alexis held up her glass of Coke with a grin. "Here's to education."

Trey offered up his slice of pizza to the toast. "Here's to real food." He stuffed the entire piece into his mouth and chewed with his eyes closed.

Gabriel raised an eyebrow at K'aia's matched enthusiasm for the twenty-inch-diameter deep-dish pan on the table. "What have you two been eating?"

K'aia paused her demolition of the pizza and shuddered. "Our own cooking." She snagged another slice and gazed at it lovingly. "Can't tell you how glad I am that the ship has a food printer. None of our favorite places to eat exist in this reality, and we both *suck* at food prep. I swear, I'd rather live on nutritional substitutes than spend another minute preparing misery on a plate."

Gabriel's eyebrows went up. "It can't have been that bad, surely?"

K'aia waved him off with her pizza slice. "Bad enough that we're going to change the subject in case it ruins this pizza by association."

Trey nodded at Gabriel, speaking around his mouthful of cheesy yumminess. "Mmmf, 'gree." He got up to get himself a drink from the dispenser. "We had no idea how good we had it back home, with parents who know how to make food that doesn't make you cry while you're eating it. The food printer is a precious luxury."

Alexis finished her bite and sat back to wipe her fingers on her napkin. "Not just the food printer. The *Gemini* has everything we need to make it a home away from home."

Trey gulped half of his milk and put his cup down with a clatter. "Good, because our base is not the homiest." He screwed up his face. "Actually, it doesn't have much of anything."

"That's not true," K'aia countered. "It had plenty of junk lying around when we moved in." She lifted a shoulder at the look of interest from Alexis and Gabriel. "Previous tenants left a bunch of lab equipment and other stuff. We moved it to the basement so it's not under our feet. It's a great place to hide out. You'll see."

### Belv'th, First City, Warehouse District, Team Base

Gabriel entered the warehouse floor from the hangar and let out a low whistle. "It's spacious. We won't run out of room to..." He furrowed his brow. "Actually, I'm not sure what we need all of this space for."

Alexis shoved him as she skipped past. "You're kidding, right? You haven't forgotten the reason we're here, have you? We need a base. This will be perfect for our APA, every base needs an active participation area. We'll get the basement fitted out for R&D." She brightened at the idea of setting up a lab of her own. "I love this place already."

Gabriel shook his head, picturing how the room they were in could be divided into different training areas. "No. I haven't forgotten, but this isn't what I expected. Mom has threatened us with military school so often that I was prepared for rigorous structure."

Alexis patted Gabriel's shoulder and pointed to a group of crates by the wall. "I think that's the point. We expected realistic *scenarios* to follow, and instead, we are in an alternate reality with no guidance for our goals." She took a seat on one of the crates and folded her hands in her lap as she spun out her reasoning. "We are free to choose our own paths through the gameworld. You want to go to military school? We just have to find one."

"That's exactly what I'm talking about." Gabriel dropped onto the crate next to Alexis with a long sigh. "How do we know what the right path is? I don't want to let Mom and Dad down."

Alexis snorted. She could always rely on Gabriel to cut right to the heart of the matter. "I feel the same, but what does Mom always say about failure? This world is laid out just for us. We're smart, and we're trained for pretty much anything. What do you *want* to experience?"

"I don't *know*," Gabriel shot back, his imitation of his sister's tone a little sharper than he'd intended. "I'm sorry. You're right. As long as we make our best effort, our parents will be proud of us whatever we choose."

Alexis smiled at Trey as he entered the warehouse floor. "In the meantime, we should focus on making this space work for us."

## 5

## Belv'th, First City, Team Base (six weeks later)

Trey grunted in frustration and threw his staff to the mat. "This isn't *working*. I'm not getting any stronger or faster. Not any more than I would be from all the training, anyway. I don't think Eve has given me the nanocytes yet."

Gabriel lowered his batons and sighed. "Probably not. You wouldn't want to experience the change all at once. There's a reason people are usually put into an induced coma while they're undergoing the transformation. You have to train; the changes will come."

Trey dropped to a cross-legged position and slumped until his forehead was touching the mat. "If you start quoting Mister Miyagi at me, I swear I'll delete every Earth movie we have that was made before the advent of CGI. Alexis owes me a favor."

Gabriel raised an eyebrow. "What, even the first *Terminator* movie? You love that one." He laughed at Trey's look of dismay and offered him a hand. "I'm not going to chew you out with old lines."

Trey got to his feet and they walked over to the half wall at the edge of the mat to retrieve their water bottles. "I'm bored. All we do is train, work on the base, and laze around watching movies. Vigilantism is starting to look attractive to me as a way to get some excitement."

Gabriel snorted his water. "Being chased through the streets by angry mobs isn't the only way to get your adrenaline fix." He had no problem with switching up their routine, just not flying by the seat of their pants while they did so. "Working as a specialist team to stop crimes in progress is not unappealing as a practical exercise."

Trey picked up his wrist-holo and fastened it on. "Alexis showed me how to tap into the city's communication network. It shouldn't be too hard to find the law enforcement channels and listen in."

Gabriel shook his head. "No. We do this right. Preparation is key to success; you know that."

Trey threw up his hands and flashed a bright grin at Gabriel. "Yeah, but you're not thinking of the fun factor."

Alexis and K'aia rushed in through the double-door.

Alexis waved a sheet of holopaper as she dashed over to the workout area. "You're not going to believe what I found in the First City News."

"*We* found," K'aia clarified, handing Gabriel and Trey each a copy of the daily news publication. "Everyone in the bazaar is talking about it."

Gabriel scanned the text of the leading story, then looked at Alexis with confusion. "What does a war two galaxies over have to do with this planet?"

"Not the war." Alexis waved her finger at the menu. "The warning about gangs of kidnappers in Second City.

We went over to check it out and found a person putting flyers up, and they told us about people getting snatched off the streets. Not cool."

Trey gaped at Alexis. "Definitely not cool. What are we going to do about it?"

"Keep reading," Alexis told him flatly. "You need to read the reports from the attack last night."

Gabriel's face darkened as he read. He crushed the newspaper in his hands without meaning to. "We have to do something about this. Can we find out where these gangs are operating out of?"

Alexis nodded. "Yeah. I've got Gemini cross-referencing every report and rumor with the spaceport records from both cities. As soon as she has something, we'll know."


## QGE *Gemini*, War Room (two days later)

Alexis sat at the oval table, a map of the quadrant open in the interactive holo display over the flat-black polymer. "Can you filter the disappearances by date?"

"Of course," Gemini replied from the speaker. The glowing white markers on the map blinked and were replaced with all the colors of the spectrum. "Reds are the most recent reports, violets are the oldest," she explained.

Alexis squinted at the sudden deluge of color. "Okay, now take out all the colors except violet." She tapped the console embedded in the table to zoom in on the cluster of markers in the galaxy one over from theirs. "This can't be a coincidence."

She opened the ship's comm. "Guys, we've got a location. How are things looking in the hold?"

Trey came back first. "I like our chances against the forces of darkness a lot better after seeing all the cool stuff your game-Mom tricked us out with. There's stuff we've only dreamed about deploying. I kinda feel sorry for the bad guys."

Gabriel's laughter rang out. "Sure, Trey. You gonna cry while you're fighting in one of these battlesuits?"

Alexis hadn't seen anything that fit the description of a battlesuit. "Show me."

An image arrived in her HUD's message function. She opened it, and her eyes went wide. "Oh my. That *is* a pretty thing. It has pretty shoulder armaments and pretty guns on the gauntlets.

"Pretty?" Trey asked.

"Pretty destructive," Alexis clarified. "Those look like Dukes' weapons to me. Are those sword hilts built into the thigh plates?"

"Just like the ones in Mom's old armor," Gabriel confirmed. "I always wanted an Etheric sword."

Alexis grinned. "I know, right? You should be able to use it after some practice."

"What about me?" Trey asked.

"NO!" all three cried at once.

"Fine." Trey huffed. "It's not like I can activate the dumb thing anyway."

Alexis winced at the hurt in his voice. "That's not a bad thing. Messing around with the Etheric is a guaranteed way to bring about a reset, and we've worked too hard to get the base how we want it to let *that* happen. Let's at least get on an objective trail before you get yourself blown to pieces."

"What do you want us to do, then?" K'aia inquired.

Alexis grinned. "We get ourselves kidnapped, of course. How else do we get a real battle?"

## Belv'th, Second City, Entertainment District

K'aia began to doubt the wisdom of their plan once they were on the streets of Second City without a single weapon at hand. "I do not like being in public without my armor," she grumped. "I like you three with your squishy flesh being unprotected even less."

"Don't sweat it," Alexis assured her. "Kidnappers don't want corpses. Come on, stay with the crowd. Hopefully, they'll be drawn to all these easy targets." She flashed a grin at the people in front when they turned to look at her. "Keep moving, nothing to see here."

The intoxicated night-goers went on their way, Alexis already forgotten in their pursuit of the next happy hour.

Gabriel spotted a furtive movement in the crowd ahead. "Look sharp. Gas canisters, eleven o'clock." More canisters rolled out into the street from the shadowy alleys. "Score. We've found the kidnappers."

People all around them panicked as others began dropping to the ground. The street was filled with confused shouts and cries of disgust as the gas caused the victims to void the contents of their stomachs before passing out.

Alexis cursed the nausea that assailed her despite the gas being rendered null by her nanocytes. "I *hate* gas. Trey, get your rebreather in. This is about to get messy."

Trey hurried to get the buds into his nostrils before the odorless, colorless gas rendered him immobile, then copied Alexis' and Gabriel's pretense of fainting. He found it almost impossible to still his reaction when he was picked up and tossed into the back of a vehicle.

He concentrated on drawing breath through the twin buds in his nostrils as a distraction from the worry of being split up from the others.

Trey chose not to inspect his thoughts about how quickly he had bonded with K'aia and the twins.

A peep through one slitted eye showed him that the kidnappers were relaxed. He could tell they had the easy camaraderie that came from long years of working together just from the way they spoke to each other.

Another few people were thrown into the back with Trey, then Gabriel landed roughly beside him.

Alexis was next. She winked at Gabriel and Trey, then shot them a panicked glance when K'aia's voice broke the silence. She tensed, ready to act at a moment's notice if it sounded like K'aia was in trouble.

There was a scuffle, then K'aia was thrown in with the rest of them, canceling the need for a one-girl riot.

K'aia laid still while the kidnappers pulled down the roller door and locked it. She didn't move until the vehicle set off. "Uuugh. I'm not as immune to that gas when it's sprayed in my face."

"K'aia, are you okay?" Alexis asked in a low voice. "Did they hurt you?"

K'aia turned her body to face the others. "I'm not injured," she ground out. "But that big guy needs a clean uniform after I puked all down it. Serves the asshat right."

Gabriel kept his ear to the bed of the vehicle, tracking their progress by the sound of the tires crunching on the road. "I know where we are," he informed them. "We just passed out of Second City, and this is a gravel road, which means we're headed for City-on-the-Lake."

Alexis asked the question on all their minds. "Why would they take us there? There's nothing but mines and villages that way."

K'aia grimaced. "Maybe that's their thing, kidnapping people to work the mines?"

"Not for long, if that's the case," Gabriel promised.

They found out soon enough when the vehicle carrying them came to a stop. They feigned unconsciousness when the door was rolled up.

The kidnappers got to work, unloading the unconscious people onto waiting antigrav pallets.

They were taken around the building they'd been brought to and deposited on the grass at the back with the people from Second City.

The NPCs were waking up, some faster than others. Gabriel took that as his cue to sit up and get a look at their surroundings. "Whoa. This definitely wasn't here before."

Trey spat to get the cottony taste out of his mouth and tilted his head to look at the tower and the building wrapped around the base of it. "What is that?"

"The building is an elevator," Alexis told him. "It will let out above the atmosphere, where a ship will be waiting to take us to our destination. I just can't see why they would go to all that expense. This isn't the most cost-effective method of getting cargo into space."

K'aia gazed up the needle, getting a reminder of her nausea as she lost the construction in the clouds. "It's a bit much, don't you think?"

Gabriel noted the identical awe in the expressions of the people around them. "I don't know. It's not like they can use the ports." He turned away from the space elevator and tried to estimate how many people there were with them. A couple of hundred, he was sure. "I think this is connected to the war we read about. The question is, where is the militia based?"

"Over there," Alexis interrupted, nodding at the black-clad figures standing around, their eyes constantly roaming over the crowd. "Soldiers. We're being shipped out."

Trey found himself far out of his depth. "What do we do? Leave the planet to chase this objective chain?"

It was a tense moment for Alexis. "We have to agree as a team, and there's not much time."

More soldiers appeared from the elevator building. They shepherded the group inside with their rifles, ignoring the questions of the people.

Gabriel furrowed his brow. "I think we take it. Either we found an organization to take down or a military to train us."

K'aia grinned. "Whichever it is, it's going to be an adventure."

Trey nodded, a smile spreading over his face. "Yeah. It beats the heck out of hanging around the base."

Alexis nodded. "Looks like we're going traveling. Wait, what about Gemini? We can't take the ship. She'll be alone until we return here."

Gabriel's eyes were unfocused for a moment. "I've told her we're going offworld. She's not happy about being left behind, but she said she will keep the base safe until we get back."

Alexis checked with the EI and confirmed she would be fine. "Okay, then. Let's start the scenario."

They integrated themselves with the line heading into the elevator and took their seats once they were inside. The line moved placidly, since the armed soldiers all around put any ideas of escape out of the question.

The elevator took them to the platform Alexis had predicted, where they were ushered into a huge room and left to mix with the people already there.

Alexis dialed out the background noise that hit them on entering. They were standing in a crowd of a hundred thousand or more, all packed between the doors and a stage at the other end of the room.

Gabriel and Trey drank in the different dialects. The NPCs spoke every language their translation software knew, mingled with untold indecipherable others.

Gabriel frowned in disappointment. "They don't know any more than we do."

Alexis and K'aia were focused more on what was coming next.

K'aia pointed at the stage. "What's going on over there?"

Alexis started making a path through the crowd. "I don't know, but the NPCs are all heading that way. Let's go find out."

They gravitated toward the stage, coming to a stop a short way from the blinding footlights. The team looked up as one when the space was lit by floodlights somewhere above their heads. Six extremely tall uniformed aliens of varying species emerged from the wings and made their way to the center of the stage.

The tall aliens turned slowly and faced the crowd, then spoke as one.

"Welcome to whichever version of an unpreferable afterlife your species subscribes to. You have been given a chance to repay your debt to society by dedicating your lives to a greater cause, one that does not benefit any single individual. The survival of civilization. You will be assigned a base, and provided with training. Then you will be shipped to the front lines, where you will fight—or you will die."

The mysterious aliens on the stage vanished, followed by the stage itself the next moment.

K'aia growled. "There goes our chance to take out the bad guys."

Alexis shook her head. "That was all smoke and mirrors. A trick," she clarified for Trey. "They were holograms."

"Sounds like we got conscripted." Gabriel speculated on the difference between this and the method by which Bethany Anne grew her military. "That explains where all the missing people have been taken."

Trey glanced around at the NPC soldiers. "I wonder who they want us to fight?"

Alexis narrowed her eyes as the armed soldiers moved to resume herding the new conscripts. "It doesn't matter. Like I said, we have to see the scenario through now that we've begun."

"We're drawing attention," Gabriel murmured. "We need to move."

They stayed together as the soldiers ushered them through the corridors to a space lined with large windows.

The soldiers ordered the conscripts to form a line, deferring to the sergeant at the desk in front of the open airlock.

Alexis examined what she could see of the hull of their transport through the windows as the line for boarding inched forward. "I hope our ship is safe while we're gone. I don't like leaving Gemini behind."

"Agreed," Gabriel told her. "But it's not practical to have her follow us. I guess I understand why Mom and Dad haven't wanted to take us with them all the time. Gemini doesn't have the tools to cope with dangerous situations."

They reached the head of the line, where they were given a band for their wrists before they entered the ship.

Trey swept his gaze to the soldiers at either end of the concertinaed airlock corridor. *This sucks,* he thought.

Alexis stalled a step. *Trey! I heard that!*

Gabriel nodded. *Me too.*

Trey tried thinking his reply. *Did I get an ability finally? Does that mean Eve has given me the nanocytes?*

*Could be,* Alexis agreed.

*Trust you to get the ability to keep on talking,* K'aia teased.

One of the soldiers encouraged them to keep moving with the butt of his rifle.

Trey shot the soldier a dirty look and kept walking. *Bethany Anne spoke mind-to-mind with me at the gala,* he explained.

*So it makes sense that would be the first thing to get activated.* Gabriel resisted the urge to headbutt the sneering soldier who scanned their wristbands at the ship's hatch.

The way ahead was also lined with armed guards. They moved whenever one of the conscripts looked to be getting ideas about breaking free of the procession.

*Thing is,* K'aia told him, *we're going to be inside this can, and we have no way to keep anything else that develops hidden from our friends here.*

Alexis nodded minutely, her attention on the soldiers. *That's my concern. The first few times Gabriel and I accessed the Etheric were disasters.* She narrowed her eyes as they entered an enormous hold filled with rows of what looked like Pod-docs standing on end. *Oh.*

*What, oh?* K'aia asked. *What's with the gloomy look?*

Trey had bigger concerns. *Never mind that. What's with all the equipment in here?*

*They're putting us in stasis,* Gabriel informed him. *Which means we're being taken farther than the next galaxy over.*

Alexis kept moving despite the sinking feeling she had. *I don't know if we're ready for this. All our gear is back at the base.*

K'aia grunted. *I'm not getting gassed again, so don't even suggest that we force a reset.*

Alexis shook her head. *I wasn't planning to. We made our choice, and we have to deal with it. Besides, it's Eve's plan. Think of Trey's nanocytes kicking in just now; this has to be a check-point. We'd just reset back here.*

They reached the head of the line, where the soldiers were joined by a group of technicians who steered them into the stasis Pods without making eye contact or speaking.

Trey gulped as the door sealed him in. His mind ran

wild with thoughts of the changes his body was going through.

He knew enhancement was different for each person. That his nanocytes were working inside him to unlock the ultimate version of Baka-ness he had hidden in his DNA.

Trey imagined himself with rippling muscles and the ability to toss his uncle out on his ass. The fantasy soothed him, since it would be his reality once he got out of the game.

It was the rest of his burgeoning powers that were the mystery. He was the first Baka to be gifted with nanocytes, so nobody knew for sure what they were going to do to him.

What would he wake up to?

6

---

Alexis woke up to a bright light raking her eyes. She lifted her arm to cover her face, only to have it pulled down again.

"Keep still, recruit," a stern voice ordered.

Alexis opened her eyes and found herself on a gurney inside a vast tent. The light burned her eyes. She squeezed them closed and willed the fuzziness in her head to clear.

Gabriel was less disoriented, but not by much. Waking up on his back when he'd been in a vertical position in the stasis Pod would do that. He caught the attention of the technician by his bed. "Where are we?"

The technician smiled sadly. "You're a soldier now. Don't ask questions; they don't like it. Just do as you are told, and you'll be fine. Now, let me see your eyes. We have to be sure the year in stasis didn't cause any damage."

The journey had taken a year? Gabriel wondered what that meant for their training. He looked around while he waited for the technician to finish checking him over.

He spotted Alexis and K'aia easily, but there was no sign of Trey's skinny behind anywhere he could see.

There was another Baka a few beds over, but he was fully grown.

The Baka frowned at Gabriel. "What the hell has happened to me?" he hissed in Trey's voice.

Gabriel's mouth fell open when he realized the Baka *was* Trey. "You grew some," he managed to reply.

The technician shook her head. "No fraternizing. You're good. Make your way to the parade ground, recruit."

Gabriel thanked her and made his way out of the tent. He was joined by the others as he stepped into the hot, damp air of the planet they were on.

K'aia sniffed and growled. "Great. My braid is going to be a nightmare to maintain in this humidity."

"Check out my guns!" Trey enthused. He flexed his arms. "I should charge admission for the show."

Alexis rolled her eyes, chuckling at Trey's joy. "You look like your uncle Li'Orin."

Trey patted his stomach. "I've got a good few pounds to gain before *that's* true."

They walked over to a grassy knoll that separated the expansive, graveled parade ground and the collection of tents and long, low, prefabricated buildings they'd just left.

Trey scanned the tents dotted around between the buildings, then turned to scrutinize the activity around the parade ground. "This must be a dedicated training facility."

Alexis snorted, stepping off the grass onto the gravel as the sound of multiple staff instructors ordering recruits to fall in drifted across the parade ground toward them.

"You're a smart cookie. At least there *is* some training. I was starting to worry we were going to be thrown straight into battle." She waved a hand at the gravel. "Come on. We'd better get on with it."

They followed Alexis, glancing speculatively at the groups forming as they walked across the parade ground. "This one?" Gabriel suggested, indicating a smaller group of around twenty NPCs of varying species.

"Good enough for me," Trey agreed.

"What now?" K'aia asked once they were in a loose formation with the NPCs.

"'What now,'" a bulky blue alien in a light-tan officer's uniform yelled into K'aia's face, "is that recruits will not speak unless ordered to."

K'aia headbutted the officer purely out of instinct, cutting her forehead on the horn protruding from his face. Her eyes widened when her carapace was suddenly filled with dancing red laser dots. "Dammit…"

The parade ground echoed with reports of gunfire as every NPC wearing a guard uniform fired on K'aia.

Gabriel and Alexis grimaced.

"Not the best way to go," Alexis supplied.

Trey watched in horror as K'aia's body was jerked around by the impacts of multiple shots. "She can feel that!"

Gabriel lifted a shoulder. "Nah, it only hurts for a minute, then shock kicks in, and it's no worse than being punched."

Trey's reply was cut off by the void descending.

· · ·

**Attempt #2**

A blink later, they were back on the training ground on the grassy verge they'd been standing on a few moments before.

K'aia held up her hands. "My bad."

Trey snickered. "Yeah, even I know that attacking an alien with the ability to impale you on his face is a bad idea."

*Yeah, let's avoid* him *this time,* Alexis snarked, swerving to avoid the officers altogether as she led them back onto the parade ground. *We should stick to mental communication when the officer NPCs are around. Keep our heads down. Try to keep your humor to yourself, Trey. This is going to be a very long game otherwise.*

Trey wrinkled his nose as they headed back toward the group they'd chosen. It was going to be a *very* long game for him if everyone had to be so serious the whole time.

He was still in shock at K'aia's death. The authenticity of the scenario was beyond anything he'd expected. The smell was what had done it, he decided. That, and the heat. He'd never been in a game where you could taste the air. Even holomovies didn't have immersion like this.

The officer K'aia had overreacted to strode out in front of the loose ranks, his face in the air, ignoring the bewildered recruits and the staff trailing behind him alike.

*Oh, look. It's my loudmouth friend,* K'aia grumbled. *I hope he falls flat on his stupid face and gets that horn stuck in the ground.*

*Why has he even got that?* Alexis pondered, finding it an effort to keep her face straight. *It's about as useful as an appendix. We should have risked it and reset before we got on that ship.*

*Yeah, but hindsight isn't any good to us now,* Gabriel reasoned. *We need to play out the scenario.*

The officer made it to the podium front and center of the recruits without karma answering K'aia's prayer. He cleared his throat and spoke into the microphone on the podium. "Welcome to your new lives. If you are fortunate enough to catch my attention for a positive reason, you will address me as General Kispin. This is the Corral, where the dregs of the many societies you hail from are broken and rebuilt into elite weapons to be used against our mutual enemies."

He looked out with a solemn expression. "Many of you will not survive the selection process. Those who do not die will be ranked according to ability. The top one percent of those who pass will be assigned to Zenith Unit, where you will fight well and serve your people with honor in return for your freedom."

The general paused to allow the information to sink in. He grasped the sides of the podium and turned his head from side-to-side, looking out over the recruits without a drop of mercy in his gaze. "However, if you cross my path for anything other than excellence, expect to be met with disappointment. You do not want to disappoint me, or any of the personnel at this base. You have no purpose other than to survive to fight the next battle. *Any* failure to obey the staff instructors will result in undesirable conse-quences for the whole unit." He released the podium and straightened his spine, looking off into the sunset at the mouth of the valley. "I wish you all luck."

With that, the general stalked off the parade ground, his personal staff following like a pack of undersized dogs at his heels.

The staff instructors stepped forward and began splitting the fifty-deep super-phalanx into more manageable units.

Trey took it all in with growing anger, feeling so far out of his depth that he feared being swept away in the undertow. *How are you all taking this so calmly? We're prisoners.*

*Not prisoners,* Gabriel modified. *Recruits. We're not free to leave, but we will be provided for and trained. I bet Aunt Tabitha's class is going to be like a vacation compared to what we're about to experience. Don't sweat it. We'll get through this together, as a family.*

Alexis smiled and patted Trey's arm. *It's a shame your cousins couldn't be here to experience this. You've got us to watch your back.*

It wasn't news to Trey that he'd missed out on part of life as a Baka thanks to his family. *I can't wait to see what my body can do now.*

*It could take a while to get used to,* K'aia countered. *I was a bit wobbly after my enhancement.*

*I'm not worried about that. What if I suddenly start shooting energy balls or something? I'm nervous,* Trey admitted.

Alexis moved the subject along, seeing the officer headed their way. *Your body gains every skill you train for in here, so make the most of it. Think of this as an opportunity to show your family what they missed out on, and think on how much they'll regret treating you badly when we all get out of here and you kick their asses into shape.*

The staff instructor ordered their section of the phalanx to break off and they began moving.

The team shuffled along with the NPCs, going with the flow.

The SIs yelled instructions, waving their arms to direct the disarrayed ranks toward the largest of the prefab buildings. "Stay in line. Remain with your unit. You will be assigned a barracks after you leave the requisitions building."

The continuous line eventually ended in the aforementioned building, where they were each handed a tied bundle containing two sets of black uniform clothing, two sets of underwear and socks, a pair of boots, a shower bag, a towel, a pillow, and a set of sheets.

Trey paid attention to everything he saw, managing for once to keep his mouth shut until they had been escorted to one of the mid-sized prefab buildings, along with sixteen other recruits.

The officers he understood the reason for. He wasn't certain what to think about their supposed teammates. They appeared to be real, but was he supposed to *treat* them like they were? How would he feel if he bonded with one and they died or turned out to be an enemy in disguise?

It was too much to comprehend for the moment. He turned his attention to the room, which held ten scaled-up double bunks, ten footlockers, and a sturdy rec table, which was surrounded on all sides by cheap-looking chairs.

Gabriel spotted Trey's slightly dazed look and steered him toward a bunk. "It's a lot to take in, right?" He tossed his bundle onto the footlocker and started making his bed. "I wish I could tell Eve what a great job she did. If it wasn't for the features she allowed, I'd have trouble telling it from reality."

"Agreed," Alexis chipped in, climbing to the bunk above K'aia's. "You okay, Trey?"

Trey furrowed his brow as he made his bed, unsure of what answer he could give when he was feeling overwhelmed by something as simple as the size of his mattress in comparison to his newly-enlarged body. "Yeah. It's just new, is all. I'll get used to it."

K'aia laid back on her bunk with her arms folded behind her head. "This place isn't so bad, but I'll wait to see what the food is like before I get too enthusiastic."

"I don't know," Alexis murmured. "I'm missing home all of a sudden. It's quiet without CEREBRO and ADAM and Winstanley and the feeds from network command..." Her voice tapered off as she drifted to sleep.

Gabriel pulled his blanket around his shoulders, settling into his pillow with a yawn. "As long as the NPCs don't get in the way of us finding our objectives, I'm peachy."

Trey laid on his back with his eyes closed after the lights went out, unable to organize the whirlwind of events that had made his real life what it was.

Without his curiosity, the situation in the Enclave on Belv'th would have come around on Devon. His initial courage had opened the door to deliverance, and persuading his cousins to accompany him to the Hexagon had been the first step on the path that had altered his people's course irrevocably and forever.

A wave of homesickness hit Trey hard.

The challenges were being away from everything he knew and the absence of his mother. Mahi' had always been within reach, even after he had come to live with the twins and K'aia at the Hexagon. His whole life, it had been just the two of them against the world.

Now they were separated by a million miles.

Trey had to stay strong and succeed for her sake.

## Morning

Alexis woke suddenly, sensing a presence outside the barracks. A moment later, the lights came on and a bell sounded from the holoscreen over the door, splitting the silence with its discordant chime. "Wake up, everyone."

"Already awake," Gabriel told her.

K'aia rolled out of her bunk. "There's someone outside."

"Just the officers," Alexis told them. She sat up and stretched, getting a better look at their new home for the foreseeable future.

In addition to everything she had seen in the brief time before lights out last night, there was also a quartet of bathroom doors along the wall opposite the door; which had a strip of holoscreen above the casement.

"Hey," the NPC in the top bunk opposite called. "I'm Sibil." The slender reptilian covered her snub nose with the back of her clawed hand and yawned. "Guess they're not big on beauty sleep here, huh?"

Alexis grinned. "I guess not." She glanced at the door as it opened and three staff instructors came into the room. "Doesn't look like we get a minute to wake up, either."

Two of the SIs marched down the center of the bunks, banging their batons against the bedposts.

The largest, a sour-faced male with a double bar on his epaulets, stood with his arms folded and his feet apart while the others performed their unasked-for wakeup call. "Rise and shine, meatsacks," he barked. "You don't want to miss chow."

Sibil's lip curled as the SIs left, revealing a double row of serrated teeth. "I should chow down on *them*," she muttered under her breath. "I wouldn't even bother with barbecue sauce."

"I already don't like them," Alexis agreed. "Don't know about eating them, though."

K'aia chuckled as she headed for the other end of the room. "I don't think we're *supposed* to like them," she called back as she went into the bathroom.

"They don't matter," Trey told them. "Like Gabriel said yesterday, we're here to become the best damn warriors we can be." He yawned as he dragged himself out of bed. "Might have figured we weren't going to get mothered, but at least we get a meal in the morning."

---

Breakfast turned out to be an odorless blob of pale-brown paste dropped into their mess tins by a catering officer with a dour expression.

The unfamiliar culinary experience was no barrier to K'aia's appetite. She marched over to the nearest table with the intent of filling her stomachs before the meal was sidetracked by the beginning of the day's training.

Alexis eyed the contents of her mess tin warily as she and Gabriel made their way over to sit with the rest of their unit. "Mmmm, nutritional substitutes. Because chewing is so time-consuming, right?"

Gabriel snickered, accidentally getting the full flavor experience. "Mercy. What do you think we have lined up?" he asked while they waited for Trey to extract himself from the line.

Alexis shook her head, contemplating the purposes of the various buildings and training areas they'd seen around the valley. "Could be anything, but my instinct tells me this "selection process" is going to start with eliminating the weakest."

"That would make sense," Gabriel concurred, doing his best to swallow his next mouthful without tasting it.

Trey joined them at the table, his opinion on the nutritional substitute clearly on par with the twins' reaction, going by the expression of revulsion he wore. "What is this stuff? It smells about as tasty as wet cardboard."

K'aia waved her spoon at him between bites. "We'll go with 'mush' and leave the questions there, huh?" She shook her head. "It's not that bad. We could be responsible for our own food."

Trey continued to contemplate the gelatinous paste in his mess tin for a moment longer before tasting the mush. "It tastes of sadness."

Gabriel shrugged. "Eh, I've had worse. Have you ever tasted overdone dinosaur meat?"

Alexis' eyes widened. "Please don't remind me about Dad's grilling obsession. Seriously."

More of the NPCs from their unit wandered over to

the long table. The main course for breakfast was complaints about rough treatment, with a generous side-serving of bitching about the slop they'd been given to eat.

K'aia poked at her food with her spoon. She found herself wishing she didn't know better than to turn down a meal when the next one was uncertain, despite her earlier assertion. "Maybe that elite squad the general mentioned gets real food."

Trey tilted his head at K'aia's suggestion. "Zenith squad?" he asked in a low voice, glancing around to make sure none of the NPCs were in earshot. "I thought the point was to take out the people running the pressgangs?"

Alexis swallowed a mouthful of the thick paste without tasting it. *We missed that chance. We've got to play this through now. This program is designed to prepare us for leadership, right? You have—* She looked away when the mess tent was bathed in light from the entrance. "Oh, *look*. It's the wake-up crew."

K'aia followed Alexis' look of mild disgust over to the three SIs who had burst so rudely into their barracks earlier.

The SIs swaggered straight over to the food line and pushed in at the front with no regard for the recruits who had been waiting.

Alexis started to get to her feet when the largest officer shoved his mess tin in the catering officer's face and yelled at them for not being fast enough at filling it. *Yeah, no. They need a lesson in humility.*

*Leave it,* Gabriel cautioned, pulling Alexis back into her seat by her sleeve. *I don't like it any better than you do, but we* don't know if we've made enough progress to pass a checkpoint yet.

*Are we supposed to sit back and watch like it's okay?* Alexis implored, folding her arms. *Look at those rejects, pushing the catering staff around. For what? We're all eating the same slop.*

Trey continued eating as though nothing were happening. He was smart enough to keep his head down and look disinterested. *This is about dominance,* he reasoned with the experience of someone who had been the youngest and smallest his whole life. *You're used to being at the top of the pecking order. You should listen to me. If we intervene, we become targets for the whole group. Nobody is getting hurt. You have to pick your battles and fight sneaky.*

K'aia nodded, forcing another spoonful of the mush down. *Eve told us this is supposed to be like real life. That means we're probably going to see some stuff you're not going to like and there will be nothing you can do about it.*

Alexis tilted her chin. *That's the kind of thinking that makes bullies think they can get away with treating people badly in the first place. I'm not going to stand for it. You have to act when you see injustice. If you don't, can you really expect anyone else to do the same?* She screwed her eyes closed and concentrated on coiling a whisper of Etheric energy underneath an abandoned mess tin on the table without tipping it. *Got it.*

*I don't think it worked,* Trey commiserated when nothing happened.

Alexis raised an eyebrow. *Watch.*

The SIs left the line, laughing loudly while the two side-kicks congratulated their ringleader on "keeping the little people in their places."

Alexis had heard enough. She released the energy, and it sprang up and upended the tin, spilling the nutritional paste in the path of the SIs.

The lead SI slipped in the pile of mushy paste and skidded backward into the second. The impact knocked both of their tins out of their hands, adding to the mess already on the floor. Their limbs got tangled as they crashed to the ground, taking out the third SI with their tumble before the leader had registered they weren't making it out of this with their dignity intact.

Every recruit in the mess tent burst out in uncontrollable laughter as the three SIs lost their footing and landed in the slippery mess.

Trey snorted, unabashed by his glee at the disaster Alexis had caused for the bullies. *I take it back; this is too funny! What did you do?*

Alexis slapped the table, cackling along with the rest of their dormmates. *Well, there's this saint. We call her "Payback—"*

"*WHAT* IS THE MEANING OF THIS?"

Every NPC, human, Yollin, and Baka in the mess tent turned to the thunderous bellow that came from the exit.

*Ohhh, now we're for it,* K'aia groaned as General Kispin glared at the SIs, waiting for an answer. *This guy is a sadist.*

The SIs stood at attention and tried not to show how undignified they felt with smears of nutritional substitute making them look as though they'd soiled their trousers.

The leader stepped forward and pointed an accusatory finger at the recruits. "One of *them* did this, sir."

The general cast a repulsed glance at the SIs and pointed at the exit. "Get to your barracks and clean up." He leveled his angry orange glare on the recruits before turning on his heel and stalking out of the mess tent. "Outside, all of you. Transition is over."

K'aia wasn't sorry to leave the remainder of the mush. She dumped her mess tin in one of the collection bins and waited for the others to dispose of theirs.

They ducked out of the tent into the bright morning light, which revealed the base in its entirety. Gabriel took the lead, heading away from the row of tents toward the parade ground on the opposite side from the prefab barracks.

Alexis sensed that something was off. She drifted a few steps from the others, reaching out to find the source of the foreboding she felt.

*What is it?* Gabriel asked.

*It's gone.* Alexis closed her eyes and searched for the trail with her mind. *If it was there to begin with.*

Trey and K'aia exchanged mystified glances.

*Let's just get on with this,* Alexis conceded. *I'm ready for some action.*

## 7

Alexis dragged herself past the barracks and into the shower block in the next prefab. She was more than grateful to sluice off the thick layer of dried mud that was embedded in every fold and crease of her body and uniform.

The last eight weeks had been interesting if she looked at the time in the context of the ancient human proverb. The team had been pushed hard enough that even she and Gabriel had been challenged.

All four had been reckless or naïve enough to lose their lives at least once during the endless rotation of physical testing under intense psychological pressure. However, as the numbers of NPC recruits around them began to dwindle, each had found new reserves of determination to counter the adversity.

Alexis found the urge to reach for her connection to technology was beginning to pass. What she missed now was the comfort of a constant digital presence in the back of her mind.

Gemini came to mind often. While she and Gabriel were accustomed to having restricted access to all their advantages as part of their training, this was the longest they had been without contact with an EI since they had been given Phyrro as infants.

Alexis blanked the activity around her, too exhausted and stiff to join in the shenanigans. She tossed her clean clothing over the stall door, hit the shower button as she kicked the door closed, and slumped under the hot water without bothering to undress. "It's easier this way," she told herself, closing her eyes as the hot water ran over her hair. "I can sleep while I get clean, and my laundry gets done."

"Sure, and your ass will be chapped for the next week," Sibil called from the next stall. "Rookie mistake."

Alexis raised her eyebrow without opening her eyes. "What do you know about rookie mistakes?" she replied a little more archly than she would usually treat a fellow recruit. "You've been here as long as I have."

"You want to see my chapped ass?" The side of the stall wobbled, and a pair of scaly buttocks topped by a short, thick tail appeared over the top. "See? Nasty, ain't it?"

Alexis regretted opening her eyes. "Totally." She sighed as she began stripping her uniform off, now that the water had softened the mud enough for her to undo the fastenings without tearing them off by mistake. "You should put something on that. Like some pants."

The derriere disappeared, and there was a scramble before Sibil's stubby snout replaced it. "Maybe I will. Or maybe I'll keep airing it until it heals since it bothers you so much."

Alexis waved a finger over herself to indicate her half-dressed state. "Whatever you need. Want to give me some privacy here?"

Sibil tilted her head back and hissed, "Privacy. *That's* a good one. Want me to turn your sheets down while I'm at it, your Highness?"

Alexis forced her cramped fingers apart and manifested an energy ball. "Look, Sibil, you're fun on an ordinary day. I just spent the last twelve hours up to my armpits in stinking mud with my pack held above my head. My tolerance for humor is less than zero right now."

"Whatever." Sibil gave Alexis a sour look and got down. "No need for the light show."

"Don't worry about Alexis," Trey called from the open shower opposite the stalls. "She just hates getting dirty." He caught the soap that came flying over the door of Alexis' stall and began lathering his fur with it. "Thanks! I don't know why you're not enjoying this. We're outdoors, and we're learning. Who cares if we're not getting a break?"

"Wash your enthusiastic mouth out," Alexis grumbled. "Nobody could enjoy getting bested by the SIs for two whole months without a break."

"But it's a 'learning experience,' remember?" Trey launched a spray of water at Alexis' stall, catching K'aia instead as she walked through the showers with a huge towel wrapped around her braids.

K'aia screamed in surprise and threw the soaked towel at Trey. "You're an ass, Trey. I *just* got my braid dry!"

Trey grinned as he batted the towel out of the air. "You missed a spot. I was just helping." His attention was stolen by three other recruits calling a greeting as they entered the shower block. "What's with them? They haven't spoken a word to us since we got here, and now they're getting chatty?"

Gabriel looked at the NPCs. "It's the game progressing. You'll get to know the characters. When you've been in the gameworld for a while, you'll forget they're not real."

Alexis came out of her stall in a clean vest and leggings and grabbed a towel to rub her hair dry. "Normally we have our party—that's everyone playing—and we team up against the NPCs. That's those guys."

Trey got out of the shower. "So they're just *there*? Do they have a purpose?" He shook himself vigorously, spraying everything in a six-foot radius with fine rain.

One of the recruits, a scarred Shrillexian, objected. "Damn right, we have a purpose." He mimed holding a rifle. "Point and shoot, same as you, ya dumb furball."

Trey raised his eyebrows at the Shrillexian's back. "Friendly guy."

"Try not to piss them *all* off," K'aia told him. "We can learn about what's coming from what the NPCs tell us. It's like having eyes all around the base."

Sibil exited her stall and walked over to the bench dividing the showers from the lockers. "You'll get used to Gorrak. He's a miserable son-of-a-space-slug, but he's always had my back when it counted."

Alexis glanced at the others. *See?* "I get that. Sounds like you've known him for a while." She dropped her towel on the floor by the bench and sat to pull on her socks and boots. "What I want to know is how long we're going to be here at the Corral. I want to find out who we're being trained to fight."

Sibil shrugged. "I know Gorrak from way back, and we know as much as you about this enemy. Hell, we're not even soldiers, we're thieves." She looked the four of them up and down. "I've been watching you guys. You look kinda...upright, or something. Like this isn't your first time following orders. You get thrown out of the military?"

A klaxon sounded, forestalling Alexis' reply. The water shut off next, bringing complaints from the recruits in the stalls.

Gabriel pointed out the clock that appeared on the holoscreen. "Ten minutes. What do you think, lights out?"

"I'm sick and tired of being told when I can eat, sleep, and even take a dump," Gorrak growled, heading for the exit. "I'm going to look for a way out. Who's with me?"

Sibil grabbed his arm. "Be sensible, Gorrak. They've got weapons. You saw them shoot that recruit when we first got here."

Trey was mystified as to why the game characters were going through this...script? It fascinated him how realistic their emotions appeared to be. He zoned out a little, his eyes darting between Sibil and Gorrak as the exchange became heated.

K'aia stepped in to pull Trey away. "Whatever you're going to do, you can decide without any of us. We're taking our behinds to the barracks to get some rest before the next round of training begins."

Sibil tugged on Gorrak's arm. "Come on. We'll be out of here in a few more weeks, right? You can hold out until then."

. . .

**Assault Course, Outer Quadrant (three weeks later)**

K'aia panted as she sprinted along the path up the mountain with her NPC partner held securely across her shoulders. "How you doing up there?" she asked, hearing Gorrak's stomach complain at being jolted repeatedly.

"Just keep running," the Shrillexian barked, the tremulous edge to his rough voice causing him to sound somewhat fragile. "I don't care if I'm sick all down your back, just don't lose our lead. Alexis and Sibil are right behind us."

K'aia vaulted a pile of scree, bending her knees slightly as she landed to absorb the impact. "Yeah, well, I'm gonna mind if you mess my uniform up. Keep your damned mouth shut, Gorrak."

Alexis flashed by with her partner, the feather-boned Sibil, who called, "Eat our dust, suckers!" then started cackling.

Gorrak groaned at Sibil's boasting. "What's the point of earning a head start when she's just going to beat us to every obstacle?"

K'aia rolled her eyes. "We've still got five kilometers to go before we get to the next obstacle. Quit your whining, or I'll throw your ass down this mountain and take the penalty for dropping you." She shifted Gorrak's weight across her shoulders and put on an extra burst of speed to bring the Shrillexian's grumpery to an end. "Happy now?"

"I'd be happier if you shut up and ran faster," Gorrak bitched.

. . .

**Lower Atmosphere, Personnel Carrier**

Gabriel waited in line behind Trey to make his high-altitude jump. They were near the back of the line, thanks to Trey's enthusiasm when the SIs had revealed the exercise was to be air-to-ground transfers.

He checked his exosuit's systems, making certain everything was in the green. The connections between his skinsuit and the mech body were responding as intuitively as any he'd trained in outside of the game.

Trey turned to look at Gabriel through the back of the clear bubble over the cockpit. The Baka's mouth moved without a word escaping the soundproof cabin of his mech.

*Turn on your HUD,* Gabriel instructed. Trey's constant state of excitement amused him, but he was pessimistic for his friend's chances of completing today's training exercise without dying. *We'll be able to see each other on camera. Follow my lead.*

Trey looked blankly at the controls. *How do I switch it on?* He blinked in confusion when the display lit up, indicating the button to press. *Oh, got it.* Gabriel appeared in the corner of his display a moment later. *What next?*

Gabriel shuffled around Trey's mech, switching places so he was ahead of him in line. *I'll go first. Do what we practiced on the ground. Follow the instructions in your HUD. Don't panic.*

The terrain map came up in their HUDs as they slowly shuffled their mechs to the head of the line.

Trey worked it out quickly enough. *We're headed for a beach?*

Gabriel nodded, making a last adjustment to his thruster rig as he stepped up to the door to make his jump. *Looks like it. Be ready to fight when you land. There's no way it's going to be a simple drop.*

The SI manning the door wasn't giving the recruits too long to gather themselves before he helped them out of the hatch with a little shove from his mech's clawed foot.

Gabriel didn't give the SI the pleasure. He pushed off from the hatch, pressing his mech's arms to its sides as the air resistance rushed to meet his suit.

Time became irrelevant as adrenaline stole his ability to process anything but the moment. The sensation of freefalling toward the surface with only the six by five by six metal and plastic shell to protect him should the mech malfunction brought everything around him into crystalline focus.

Gabriel opened the mech's arms, slowly shifting its body until he was in a position to deploy the thrusters. He checked around for Trey as he stabilized, seeing in his HUD cam that he was still in the aircraft, hovering at the hatch with a dubious expression. *Jump before the SI pushes—*

Too late. The SI lifted his mech's foot and kicked Trey's mech out of the hatch.

Trey screamed in surprise at the sudden ejection. He windmilled his arms and legs erratically in a hopeless attempt to regain control, obeying his body's instinct instead of deploying his thrusters as his HUD was telling him to.

The mech flailed in response, plummeting toward the sand in an uncontrolled dive.

Gabriel landed at a run. He came to a stop on the wet

sand and looked up at Trey's mech looping toward the ground. He hoped Eve was getting a kick out of watching Trey try to get control of the mech.

Trey's heart beat out of his chest, clarity eluding him as his mech's head hurtled toward the planet's surface.

This was it. He was going to die.

He was overcome with relief when his mech kicked into emergency mode and the thrusters shot him upward in an attempt to avoid a crash.

Trey whooped with relief when the ground receded almost as rapidly as it had loomed in his sights.

However, his problems weren't over.

Trey's last thought as his mech slammed into the personnel carrier in a ball of flames was that it was a good thing he wasn't doing this for real.

---

The day ended over generous helpings of some pink nutritional substance and a thorough retelling of the day's happenings inside the mess tent, followed by the short walk back to the barracks.

Sibil walked with Alexis and K'aia, joining their continuing debate about the deadliest shoe to wear in a fight. "You can hide a spring blade in a low block heel."

"Your heel *is* the blade when you wear stilettos," Alexis argued. "My mother taught me there's no reason a woman can't look good *and* kick ass."

Trey glanced at Alexis doubtfully. "Yeah, but how are you supposed to kick while you're balanced on heels?"

Alexis waved him off. "I don't need that kind of negativity in my life. If my mom can do it, so can I," she declared. "Talk to me when you can walk and run all day without tripping over your bare feet.

"That's if Mom lets you wear heels," Gabriel teased.

"You forget that we'll be adults when we get out of here," Alexis reminded him. "Wait and see."

Sibil frowned. "You think we'll be released?"

Gabriel nodded. "Yeah, just as soon as we've fought whatever war is going on outside of here. It's not a bad life," he told the NPCs firmly. "If you can accept the discipline and get with the training you'll be better for it."

Gorrak raised himself onto his tiptoes and danced around Alexis and Sibil. "You females are footwear obsessed."

"Not me." K'aia scoffed, wiggling the lethal claws that tipped her toes. "All this makes me glad I come equipped with built-in weaponry."

Gabriel snickered as he passed, getting the door for them all. "That makes you sound like a cyborg."

K'aia's eyes widened. "Yeah, no. I've had all the enhancement I'm ever going to get, thank you very much."

Gorrak grunted as he swerved around K'aia to enter the barracks. "I'd take the assist. Who doesn't want to be stronger?"

---

Gabriel stared at the ceiling after lights out, waiting for sleep to come.

*You okay?* Alexis asked.

Gabriel turned onto his side. *The exercise today. It was too easy.*

*That was probably because Trey took two tries to get through the jump,* Alexis soothed, her voice small and tired. *Get some rest. You can bet we'll have an early start.*

"An early start" turned out to be an eerily accurate prediction.

Alexis was awoken by explosions outside the barracks after what felt like thirty seconds' sleep.

The barracks door burst open and a group of SIs rushed in, wearing hoods with cut-out eyeholes to conceal their identities.

The twins were out of their bunks and on their feet in half a breath, backed up by K'aia and Trey.

Sibil and Gorrak moved to widen the defense line, joining the team as the SIs attacked.

The SIs yelled to intimidate the recruits, jabbing them with the arc rods they carried.

The recruits reacted in various ways. Some were bewildered by the attack and went down easily, while others shook off the electricity coursing through their bodies and fought back.

"Coming through," K'aia called as she barged at the SIs.

Alexis and Gabriel acted simultaneously, pincering two of the staff instructors as K'aia charged the others head-on. The first two went down easily, taken out by the impact of K'aia's heedless tackle and their subsequent introduction to the wall.

Three more came through the door with their batons drawn, the electric nodes at the tips spitting sparks into the darkness.

K'aia chuckled darkly as the SIs advanced on her. "Guys, look at their cute little batons."

Sibil giggled. "K'aia, it's not nice to mock others for their shortcomings."

Alexis lit the dorm with an energy ball, creating another to flick at the SIs. It took out their batons, leaving them open for Gabriel and K'aia while she secured the unconscious two.

Trey jumped in when another hooded figure rushed in. He knocked the SI flying with a swift, strong punch to their chest, then dashed after the instructor and kicked them in the head to be certain they stayed down. "Take *that.*"

He trussed the unconscious staff instructor with a bedsheet and dragged them over to sit against the wall with the other five officers. "What now?"

Without warning, the dorm's shutters dropped. The recruits immediately began trying to escape as the room was flooded with opaque purple gas from the air vents.

"Damn gas again!" Alexis cried. She clamped her sleeve over her mouth, gesturing for the other recruits do the same.

There was no way to protect themselves. Even the twins were affected by whatever chemical the SIs was dosing them with.

The NPC recruits began dropping to the floor as the gas took effect.

Trey was next, slumping as his knees forgot how to be solid and his head suddenly doubled in weight.

K'aia cursed as her legs gave way. She staggered another

three steps and went down with a crash, plowing through the rec table as she fell.

Alexis met Gabriel's gaze as the gas overwhelmed them both. She slid to the floor, unable to help but notice how pretty the noxious cloud was as her eyes closed.

## 8

Alexis woke and found herself unable to move. Her eyes and limbs were heavy, but her nanocytes were rapidly clearing whatever drug they'd all been gassed with.

Hesitant to peek at her surroundings and give away that she had regained consciousness, Alexis tested her other senses.

Gabriel's heartbeat was easy to pick out. *Gabriel, you awake?*

His reply was slurred, his mind almost-but-not-quite free of the drug.

Alexis sent calming energy through their mental link, and also to K'aia and Trey, who were still fully under, then continued her tentative sensory exploration of the area while she waited for her brother to wake up.

There were more heartbeats, sluggish and even. The other recruits from their unit. She heard muffled movement in the distance—doors closing and muted conversation.

That told Alexis they were in an occupied building. She

could smell antiseptic, meaning it was most likely the medical facility. Alexis couldn't read any minds in the immediate area, but that didn't mean there weren't any guards outside the door or cameras watching them.

Gabriel had almost broken through the drugged sleep.

She cracked one eyelid a fraction, confirming that the only occupants in the sterile room were her team and the other recruits from their unit. She couldn't see a camera anywhere in her line of sight, so she opened her eyes a tiny bit wider to get a better look.

Gabriel stirred, drawing her attention.

*You're awake!* Alexis couldn't keep the relief out of her inner voice.

Gabriel's first thought on regaining consciousness was for his sister. *Alexis, are you okay? Where are we?*

*I'm good. We're in the medical facility, I think,* Alexis replied. *We need to get out of here. Trey is going to totally freak out if he wakes up to this.*

Gabriel murmured his agreement. *Do you think K'aia will be okay?*

Alexis considered. *Yes. She's got Mom's and Dad's training to rely on. We've done so much abduction training since the mall world, I know we're fine. I'm just concerned about Trey. Even with all his hardships with his family, he's lived a pretty sheltered life.*

Trey was still out cold for the moment. K'aia was just beginning to stir, murmuring groggily as her drug-induced dream faded.

Gabriel tried unsuccessfully to get up to soothe K'aia, finding he had the same issues with mobility Alexis had discovered upon waking. *I'm tied down. Give me a few minutes.*

Alexis gritted her teeth, then dislocated her thumb and pulled her hand out of the metal cuff chaining her to the bed. *Race you.*

Gabriel looked over when Alexis hissed softly. He didn't feel much like causing himself unnecessary injuries. Instead, he grasped the chains of his restraints with both hands and snapped them with a sharp twist and a tug.

*Showoff,* Alexis teased, hopping down from the bed to look for something to cut Trey free. *Get K'aia loose since she's almost awake. I've got Trey.*

Gabriel grabbed a laser scalpel from the counter and started cutting through the synthetic straps binding K'aia to the bars on the sides of her bed.

K'aia's eyes fluttered open while he was leaning over to cut the final strap. "What happened?"

Gabriel put a finger to his lips. *Looks like we were more of a handful than they were prepared to deal with, so they gassed us. We've been taken to the medical facility.*

K'aia inched her aching body forward until all four of her feet were hanging off the side of the bed. *Can I get a hand?*

*Yeah, here.* Gabriel assisted K'aia in getting off her side and onto her feet again. *You good?* He smiled when she gave him a nod to confirm. *I'm going to help Alexis get the other recruits loose. Keep watch while we get everyone up.*

*Got you.* K'aia shook the fatigue from her body and shuffled over to guard the door while Gabriel and Alexis freed the rest of their unit.

Alexis pondered the logistics of getting twenty bodies

through an occupied building without being seen by the medical personnel or any guards.

Gabriel wiggled his eyebrows. *What would Mom do?*

Alexis cast a doubtful glance at her brother. *Mom wouldn't get caught in the first place, and if she* did, *she would just tear the place down.*

Gorrak glowered at the door, rubbing his head to try to shift the dull throb left behind by the gas. "We gonna get out of here, then?" He shrugged at the look Alexis and Sibil gave him. "What? You can't think it's a good idea to stick around after the SIs attacked us like that."

Gabriel furrowed his brow. "We weren't attacked. It was an exercise, which we failed."

Trey's lip curled. "What are you saying? That we were supposed to let them drag us out of there?"

Gabriel lifted a shoulder. "Maybe? This is a sticking point for us all in some way. We have to be able to make it through if we're captured by the enemy."

K'aia shuddered. "They were quick enough to incapacitate us with the gas when we fought back. I'd call that a fail."

Alexis frowned as she undid the restraints on the last recruit. "You think it was supposed to be interrogation training and we messed up?"

"I don't care what it was," Gorrak cut in, heading for the door. "It was bad enough luck in the first place when we were forced to choose between this and hard labor."

The majority of the group agreed with Gorrak.

K'aia blocked Gorrak's way. "You can't go out there. We need to find a way out without being seen."

The twins turned to look at Trey.

Trey didn't like the attention one bit. "Why do I get the feeling you're about to say something I'm not going to like?"

Alexis shrugged. *Your game, your call.*

*Stay or leave?* Gabriel asked.

Trey was torn. *Let me think.* He frowned, wondering if this was how Mahi' had ended up fleeing to Devon. *It's impossible to decide without knowing what we were supposed to do in the first place.*

*I know, but that's how the game works,* Alexis replied. *If you don't decide on an action, it will decide for you.*

"Indecision is still a decision," Gabriel advised. "What's it going to be?"

K'aia turned her head from the door as the recruits began putting in their two credits' worth. "If we're going, it had better be now. It looks like visiting hours just started." She indicated the small viewing window she'd been watching from. "Our favorite Short-brained Ignoramus and his dumbass squad just turned up at the staff desk. They don't look too happy."

Trey growled low in his throat. "Then we stay and face the consequences, but we teach them a lesson. Alexis is right; we have to stand up to them, or they're going to keep making our lives miserable. I'm done taking...*shit* from bullies."

K'aia chuckled at Trey's slight hesitation. "That sounded like your first real curse word."

Trey's lip curled. "It was, and it felt good. Everyone, find a weapon. Whatever you can use to defend yourselves."

Most of the recruits set to work dismantling the frame of one of the smaller beds.

Gorrak snorted at their efforts, climbing onto the counter to get to the almost-too-conveniently-placed air vent. "People like that don't learn. They find a way to come back harder, and they crush you. We've got a chance to escape, and I'm going to take it."

Sibil threw a chart at him. "Then you're as deluded as the SIs are brutal. How far do you think you're gonna get before they drag your dumb ass back here and stick your head on a pole to display as an example to every recruit on the base?"

Gorrak hesitated with his hands on the vent cover. "I hate you when you're right."

"All the time, then?" Sibil teased. "We'll find a way out of here if you're so set on it. For now, do something to help solve our problem instead of being part of it."

Gorrak sighed. "Fiiine. Everyone get out of my way." He turned and took a running jump off the end of the counter, cannonballing into the bed as the recruits scattered to clear the area.

The bed's frame, intended for holding patients human-sized or smaller, gave under Gorrak's weight.

K'aia and Sibil helped him to his feet as the recruits moved in to finish the job of tearing the frame apart at the welds.

A moment or two later, most of the recruits held a bar of some length.

K'aia cursed under her breath when the door handle turned. "Come and get us."

The door swung open, revealing an apoplectic General Kispin. The general strode into the ward with the SIs at his back, his jowls shaking from side to side in his rage. "Stand down *immediately*," the general bellowed, spraying the air with saliva. "Or be charged with mutiny."

Fully half the group obeyed instantly in fear.

Trey aimed his section of the bedpost at the beaten and bruised SIs, leaning forward as he spoke through clenched teeth. "Mutiny? They attacked *us*." He threw his weapon at the general's feet in disgust. "It's not our fault your staff is too incompetent to carry out your orders. If you're going to punish us for doing exactly what you're training us for, then just get it over with, so we can get back to preparing for the war. Sir."

The recruits winced as one.

*I didn't mean for you to speak back to the general,* Alexis contested. *Now we'll have to do the whole scenario again, and that gas sucked.*

*I don't care. He's not getting away with this.* Trey refused to drop his eyes. He tilted his chin to meet the general's gaze, making it clear that he wasn't cowed by being in a precarious position.

The general looked for a moment like he was going to run Trey through with his horn on the spot. He whipped his head around when one of the SIs let a snicker escape. "What are you laughing at?" he demanded. "You're in no less disgrace than the recruits."

The SI on the firing line held up his hands and stepped back before he was introduced to the pointy end of the general's facial appendage. "Sir, this unit has been trouble since they got here."

Alexis rolled her eyes. "You've been abusing your positions and we haven't been putting up with it, you mean," she corrected, her tone dripping with snark. "I come from a military family, and not one person I know would eat before everyone under their command had eaten their fill."

The general frowned. "This is news. However, consequences are consequences." He indicated Trey and the others with a finger. "You are assigned to punishment detail until further notice. Then we will speak."

The SI who had spoken made a sound of disbelief.

The general whirled to face the SI and laid him out with a single punch. He flexed his fingers and turned his attention to the rest of his junior officers. "Get him up from there. Damn idiot is making a mess of the place."

The SIs hurried to obey, picking up their unconscious teammate from the floor. They waited for the general's permission to leave.

The general stared at them in disgust. "The rank of Staff Instructor is a privilege, not an excuse to benefit at the expense of others. You are all hereby relieved."

"But, sir!" one of the former SIs appealed. "Where will we go?"

The general glared at the group of eight. "What do I care? You have forgotten what we are fighting for, so you're done here. If you want to redeem yourselves, I suggest you volunteer for the front lines so you can at least die with honor."

# 9

Cool, sweet air swept in periodically through a gap in the seam of the catering tent. The unpredictable, all-too-brief reprieves from the thick heat coming from the huge pans somehow made it even worse to be stuck in the tent.

Especially when the rest of the recruits were enjoying the relative freedom of being in the outdoor training areas.

"This is beyond immoral," Gorrak protested. "The officers eat like kings while we are given slop that an animal would refuse."

"The affront is being made to prepare their meals for the last two weeks," Alexis argued.

Gabriel nodded and pointed his peeler at Alexis. "Yeah."

Sibil glanced at the catering officer to make sure he wasn't looking and spat in the pot of water in the center of their circle of chairs. "Hope they choke on it."

Trey tossed the root vegetable he'd finished peeling into the pot and flexed his aching fingers before reaching for another from the bucket beside his chair. "I mean, it could have been ditch duty until full dark. Again."

Everyone groaned at the thought of *that* mind-numbing task.

Gorrak sat back and folded his arms. "Yeah, well, I'm waiting for it to come around again. I think I might have found a way off this base the last time we were out there digging. All we need is a distraction."

K'aia shook her head at the stubborn Shrillexian. "You don't quit, do you? None of us is getting off the base. Accept it already, and you'll be less crabby."

Sibil punched Gorrak's arm fondly. "Yeah, look on the bright side for a change."

Gorrak brushed her off, leaning in to talk in a near-whisper while the catering officer's attention was on the preparation of the main course. "I'm out of here tonight while the guards change shifts. I mean it, Sibil. I'm leaving whether anyone comes with me or not."

K'aia glanced at Alexis. *He seems pretty determined to leave. What if we're supposed to help him?*

Alexis looked down and frowned at the pile of peels at her feet. *I can't see Eve constructing the game that way.*

Trey half-listened to the girls, more interested in Gorrak's passionate argument for escaping the base.

The Shrillexian waved his peeler around, not caring if the catering officer noticed. "We've never been shown the enemy or told anything except that they are there. How do we know they even exist? This is a prison, plain as the nose on General Kissbutt's face."

Gabriel dismissed the statement. "That's not logical. If this is a prison, why incur the expense and risk of training us?" He held up a hand to forestall Gorrak's rebuttal. "I'm not saying you're wrong to be suspicious, I'm saying you should look elsewhere."

"You don't like having an unknown enemy," Trey guessed.

Gabriel had come to his conclusion. He pointed at Trey and nodded. "Got it in one. I think it's time to call our parents."

"Later," Alexis agreed. "We'll send a message through Eve."

"Quiet down over there," the catering officer ordered, scowling at them.


### Barracks

Alexis felt a much-missed tingle in her mind. The sensation revitalized her tired body. She sat up. "I've had a reply from Eve."

She opened the message and read the single line. "It's a text. Mom will be available to talk to us in five minutes."

Gabriel shifted his position to get a better view of the clock on the holoscreen above the door. "I was hoping it would be Mom who answered. Dad would likely tell us to follow the rules. Mom will guide us as to what's right."

Sibil sat cross-legged on Gorrak's bunk. "You have people, and they allowed you to be sent here?" Her face matched her tone of disbelief. "*Why?*"

"Our parents were the ones who sent us here," Alexis clarified. "Why do you look so horrified? This is an excellent training program, staff personality issues aside."

Sibil looked around the group, getting nods of confirmation from Gabriel, K'aia, and a slightly reluctant Trey. "What if you die?"

Trey remembered that for Sibil and the other NPCs, there was only one go-round. "We're not going to die, and neither are you. We've got each other's backs."

Alexis nodded. "Yeah, Gabriel and I have been training our whole lives. This process is demanding, of course, but compared to some of the things we've done, it's no different than an extended school trip."

Gabriel snickered. "Yeah, remember when we free-climbed that volcano with Uncle John?"

Alexis and K'aia cracked up at the reminder of the day that had started out as a pleasant hike through the game-world and ended with them running for their lives when the man met the mountain and decided to challenge it.

"Yeah. Who could forget the shock when we got to the caldera?" Alexis managed through her giggles. We only just made it out of there before the pyroclastic flow took us out."

K'aia slapped her mattress, almost bouncing Alexis onto the floor. "*Then* those predators chased us all the way back to the ship. Remember them?" She made claws with her hands and snapped her mandibles like teeth.

Gabriel's eyes crinkled as he recalled the thrill of racing to stay ahead of the pack. "Fun times."

Sibil's mouth worked for a moment before she managed to speak. "That sounds…terrifying. What hell are you four from? You have powers that look like magic, and a link to the outside. You could leave if you wanted, but you *like* it here?"

"Didn't say I liked it," K'aia replied. "But it's not the worst."

Gabriel nodded. "I'm learning, I'm good."

"Don't look at me," Trey told her, grinning at Sibil's confirmation of his initial perception of the breakneck pace humans lived at. "I've only been on the team for a short time."

Alexis shrugged. "It's really not so bad if you don't count the food. That's our world."

"The world isn't like that," Sibil refuted. "It's... It's... Gorrak, tell them." She leaned over her bunk to look around the room when he didn't reply, her face dropping when there was no sign of him among the other recruits. "Where's Gorrak?"

K'aia got to her feet when a translucent shimmer appeared in the space between the bunks, heralding their imminent call with Bethany Anne. "Wasn't he behind you when we got in?"

Sibil climbed down from her bunk, stepping straight through the shimmering air without acknowledging its presence. "I thought he was with Tornos. I'm gonna go and check the shower block."

Trey frowned at Sibil as she left, then turned to the others as the shimmer resolved into a vid-call window. "Can't she see it?"

"No," Gabriel told him. He broke into a wide grin at the welcome sight of his mother.

"Shhh," Alexis hissed. "The audio is coming through. Hey, Mom!"

Bethany Anne waved a hand in front of her. "Can you see me? We're pretty far from Devon." She leaned in for a closer inspection. "Look at you already! How long has it been in your time?"

"Just over a year and a half," Alexis replied before anyone else had a chance to speak.

"Why isn't Mahi' there with you?" Trey cut in. "Is she okay?"

Bethany Anne focused her dazzling smile on Trey. "Your mother is fine. Just caught up at the moment." Her smile grew wider. "You're filling out nicely, Tu'Reigd. I'll be sure to tell Mahi'. How's it going in there?"

Gabriel gave Bethany Anne a rundown of events so far, with Alexis, K'aia, and Trey adding context where he skipped over the details.

Bethany Anne listened with her hands folded in her lap. "So," she clarified once they had finished, "you're finding your world challenging to navigate."

All four nodded.

"We're still trying to figure out the game's *objective*," Alexis grumbled. "Never mind the level-up requirements."

Bethany Anne raised an eyebrow. "Sounds to me like you are having what is called a 'life experience.'" She waved away the twins' dour looks. "Take it or leave it. Life doesn't come with an instruction manual."

Gabriel inclined his head, taking the advice at face value.

Alexis narrowed her eyes. "That's not true, Mom. There are instructions everywhere you go."

Bethany Anne's mouth tipped up at the corner. "Oh? Then you should keep following them. Or you could forge your own path." She glanced away for a moment as someone entered the room. "I have to go. I would tell you not to leave it so long between calls, but I'm proud of your independence, even if I miss you."

Trey dipped his head. "Bethany Anne, please tell my mother I'm thinking of her?"

"Of course," Bethany Anne promised. "Goodbye, children."

With that, the window disappeared, leaving them no clearer on how to get the game moving to the next level.

K'aia sat back down on her bunk. "That wasn't much to go on."

Alexis arched an eyebrow, looking eerily like her mother for a moment. "You're kidding, right? That was practically a full briefing." She gave the others an incredulous look. "Don't any of you pay attention? With Mom, it's all about what she *doesn't* say."

Gabriel made a face. "It's always about the subtext with her, you mean. You two are just the same."

Alexis sniffed. "Then it's a good thing I'm here. She was clearly saying that we should do whatever we think is right, regardless of the rules."

Gabriel shrugged. "So, keep on as we were? What about everything we built on Belv'th? We'll be here until we're older than Dad if we get put on punishment duty every time we act on our dislike of something."

K'aia jerked a thumb at the clock. "I'd say we have a more immediate concern. Sibil hasn't come back yet, and it's almost lights out. What are we going to do?"

"We should go look for her." Trey was resolute. He headed out of the barracks without waiting for the others to offer an opinion.

K'aia glanced at the twins.

Alexis sighed and set off after Trey. "Come on. We'd better make sure he makes it back."

Trey met them halfway between the barracks and the shower block. He came to a stop, panting slightly. "They're not in there."

K'aia turned her head to stare across the parade ground at the valley mouth. "They've gone for the perimeter."

Gabriel groaned. "That's two more out of the program."

Trey frowned. "That's a bit heartless, Gabriel."

Gabriel shook his head, turning to go back to the barracks. "No, it's life. Like Mom said…" He paused, "Actually, I don't know how that's relevant here, but I'm not going to get killed and live through the last few weeks again over a couple of NPCs, even if they were entertaining."

Trey opened his arms to appeal to Alexis and K'aia.

K'aia lifted a shoulder. "You win some, you lose some," she told him resignedly, following Gabriel.

"We need to stick to the plan. We have to complete the training to get off this planet," Alexis rationalized. "I don't like it any better than you, but Gabriel is right. We'll be here forever if we don't get through the scenario."

Trey hesitated, but his instinct to stay with the group won out. He set off after Alexis, his shoulders drooping as he walked.

## 10

The next morning, Trey was subdued.

He felt like a wedge had been pushed between himself and the twins last night, and his silent preparation for the day wasn't going unnoticed.

Gabriel clapped him on the shoulder as he passed on his way to the bathroom. "It was a distraction, designed to trick us into failing the level. Let it go."

Trey wasn't sure he could. He trailed behind the others as they made their way to the mess tent, thinking about the likelihood of Gorrak risking his life on an unproven plan. It wasn't *that* unlikely. Gorrak was a typical hot-headed Shrillexian male with authority issues.

Sibil, however, was a clear thinker, the brains of their act. What would cause Gorrak to dismiss her decision, and why did he feel like they'd missed something?

Trey pushed his spoon around his mush, which was an insipid green today and tasted very much like it looked. He kept turning the problem over in his mind.

Alexis was about to remark on Trey's brooding when

she caught Gabriel's minute headshake, and then the call for morning parade sounded, ending the conversation before it had begun.

The team made their way out to the parade ground and fell in with the other recruits. The remaining staff instructors walked the lines under the watchful eyes of General Kispin, who sat taking breakfast at a table under a tree set back from the dust of the parade ground.

Alexis stood at ease between K'aia and a hulking recruit she hadn't ever spoken to, holding herself carefully to retain her outward appearance of composure despite her rising inner tension.

Trey was having less success containing his jitters than Alexis and the others. *I can't take this.*

*Trey, keep still!* K'aia hissed.

Trey glanced at her out of the corner of his eye. *How can I keep still when any moment the SIs are going to discover the unit is two bodies short?*

*That's inevitable,* Gabriel reasoned. *Stressing over things beyond your control is pointless. You might as well wave your arms and shout, "It was me!"*

The moment, however, did not come as expected.

The SIs completed their headcount and reported to the staff sergeant, same as every morning parade. The staff sergeant entered the final SIs' number in her datapad, as usual.

Every recruit on parade winced when she got to her feet and walked over to the general's breakfast table, but none dared speak.

They didn't need to. It was clear to them all that someone had absconded, and it was of no consequence which unit the deserters had been a part of. The general would punish all the recruits just the same.

The general dropped his napkin onto his plate and took the datapad. He examined the screen, then passed it back to the staff sergeant without a word.

Every eye on the parade ground was trained on General Kispin, waiting for his reaction.

The general twitched his head and the SIs assumed their resting positions around the perimeter of the ranks.

Then the general left without giving a single order.

Gabriel groaned, the involuntary noise causing the nearest SI to look around menacingly.

For once, Alexis did not chastise her brother. Instead, she spoke directly into his mind to keep the conversation private. *You thinking what I'm thinking?*

*That today was a bad day to ignore the crease in my sock?* Gabriel replied, skimming over his dismay at what they were about to endure.

*Yeah, that,* Alexis murmured. *How long do you figure they'll have us standing out here?*

*Could be days.* It was Gabriel's turn to lift his sister's spirits. *But don't sweat it. Just imagine you're first in line at the grand opening of some shiny new shoe palace.*

Alexis sniffed. *You're such a* male *sometimes, Gabriel. How about you pretend you're sitting in a hide somewhere with Dad?*

Gabriel felt his cheeks flush. *Um...*

*You ass,* Alexis teased. *That's* exactly *what you're planning on as your dissociation technique, isn't it? You know, the general does remind me a little of that dinosaur Dad was so obsessed with. Same air of slightly confused indignation. I can see why you would go with that.*

Gabriel rolled his eyes and adjusted his stance to bear his weight easily for the foreseeable future. He began to feel pressure from the crease in his sock after the first hour.

Over the next three, the pressure became a burning line across the sole of his foot. Conversation across the group link dried out, and Gabriel's world was whittled down to the sound of the other recruits' breathing and the tidal pain in his foot

*You okay?* Alexis asked, feeling the ghost of his pain.

*Mmhmm,* he replied. *I can use it. No big deal.*

By the fifth hour, he was praying he didn't have to separate his healed flesh from the sock when they were finally freed from their punishment.

The SIs moved from their posts just as Gabriel's internal clock informed him that they were entering the sixth hour. He limped after the others, hoping to be sent to the medic.

Sadly, nobody on the staff appeared to care about the wounded recruits.

Gabriel forced himself to keep walking, thinking to take care of the injury himself. The barracks was the most welcome sight he'd seen in what felt like forever. His relief was short-lived when they were ordered to the bathrooms, then to the mess tent, then straight back to the parade ground with no opportunity to tend to his raw foot.

Alexis and K'aia bookended the boys as they resumed their positions. The recruits baked in the afternoon heat, adding sunburned necks to their growing list of aches and pains.

The heat took out a few recruits as the sun dipped

toward the horizon. They were the ones not designed for long periods in the heat, the physically weaker ones who had been carried so far by their units.

Alexis bore the incessant strain on her back and legs by retreating into Kurtherian math problems she had memorized for occasions such as this as part of her endurance training.

K'aia appeared unaffected by the whole thing. She hummed a short tune in her mind every now and again, the mournful melody her only mental contact with the others.

Trey had pointedly ignored the others the whole time, stewing in his anger as a way to avoid the reality of twelve hours of standing in the same place.

Every so often, Alexis made an attempt to talk him out of his sulk, without success. She was thinking of trying again when the SIs came to attention.

Trey cut in on the group link, his mood forgotten in a heartbeat now that something was happening. *What's going on?*

*Don't get too excited,* K'aia grumbled. *Probably just another break.*

A fleet of open-topped vehicles arrived, pulling up at the side of the parade ground.

The SI acting as drill sergeant ordered the recruits to attention as General Kispin and his retinue exited the vehicles and made their way to the front of the parade at a brisk walk.

Silence so complete not even a bug could be heard blanketed the valley as the recruits waited on tenterhooks for the general to speak.

However, the general simply stood facing the ranks with his hands clasped behind his back.

Trey gave a low rumble in reaction to a low moan from another Baka, forgetting the NPCs weren't actually alive to need his comfort. *Why isn't he yelling at us?*

*I think we're beyond yelling,* K'aia deduced gloomily. *Just don't do anything to draw attention to yourself. Like talking.*

*Or breathing too loudly?* Trey snarked, the reason for his anger returning in an instant at K'aia's teasing. *How about, you all should have listened to me in the first place and we wouldn't be in this mess? I can't move without hearing how I'm going to mess things up because you're all so* experienced.

Alexis reined in the urge to bite him. *I've been nothing but nice to you.*

Trey's jaw twitched.

Gabriel intervened before it got out of hand. *Hey, now's not the time. There's something going on over there.*

They strained to see what Gabriel had spotted. A circle of SIs blocked their view of the vehicles, but there was clearly a disturbance of some kind.

Trey's heart dropped when he realized that the commotion was Gorrak resisting being moved. *Oh, no...*

The SIs overpowered Gorrak, forcing him to comply by means of repeated shocks from their arc rods. He stumbled onto the parade ground, blinded by the hood over his head and weighed down by chains.

Next came Sibil, half-carried by the arms between two SIs, followed by a few more recruits from other units in similar states.

The general stood aside as the seven recruits were lined up to face the ranks and forced to their knees.

Alexis and Gabriel risked glances at each other.

K'aia shuffled on the spot. *Just give the word.*

*We'll have to do the level all over again,* Alexis protested, sounding unconvincing even to herself.

*Does it matter?* Gabriel asked. *They're part of our unit. We don't leave anyone behind, and we* definitely *can't allow General Kissbutt to have them executed.*

*Your mother is right.* Trey bared his teeth and stepped out of line as the general gave the order for the SIs behind the deserters to draw their weapons. *We have to forge our own path.*

The parade ground echoed with the general's screamed outrage as the four broke ranks and dashed to save Sibil and Gorrak.

It was all the catalyst that was needed.

The parade ground broke into pandemonium as the recruits turned on the staff. The SIs plowed into them, laying about in wild abandon with their arc rods as the general screeched orders from his position of relative safety.

Gorrak broke free and killed the SIs who had shocked him with their batons before going down to the guns of the ones who had Sibil.

Trey dived to push Sibil out of the way, noting as he hit the gravel that the bullets didn't hurt anywhere near as much as he had expected.

## Attempt #2

Cool, sweet air swept in periodically through a gap in the seam of the catering tent. The unpredictable, all-too-brief reprieves from the thick heat coming from the huge pans somehow made it even worse to be stuck in the tent.

Especially when the rest of the recruits were enjoying the relative freedom of being in the outdoor training areas.

"This is beyond immoral," Gorrak protested. "The SIs eat like kings while we are given slop an animal would refuse."

"The affront is being made to prepare their meals for the last two weeks," Alexis argued, falling into the repetition of her previous actions without thinking.

Trey blinked, thrown for the moment by the reset.

This time, they didn't miss it when Tornos pulled Gorrak to the side on the way back to the barracks.

K'aia strolled over to the two Shrillexians, nodding politely at Tornos. "Nice evening for an escape, yeah?"

Tornos stepped back, holding up his hands. "Don't know what you're talking about."

Gorrak didn't see K'aia's lightning-fast right.

He *did* wonder which starship had just collided with his jaw as his legs turned to soup.

K'aia picked Gorrak up and slung him over her shoulder, nodding again to the open-mouthed Tornos. "Fair warning: go back to your barracks. You're not gonna get away."

She marched past the gathering audience into the barracks, where she unceremoniously dumped Gorrak on his bunk before getting onto her own. "That's *that* problem taken care of," she announced, folding her arm under her pillow. "Wake me up when the next pile of excreta hits the fan."

Sibil leaned over her bunk to look at Gorrak. "Why'd you do that?"

K'aia opened one eye and fixed Sibil with a hard look. "Trust me, tomorrow would have sucked in a hundred ways if I hadn't." She grunted as she turned to face the wall. "Now shush. I need to sleep."

Sibil wisely did not continue to aggravate the grouchy Yollin.

Gabriel, Alexis, and Trey were no more forthcoming. They rolled into their bunks as though they'd spent the day breaking rocks with toothpicks instead of peeling vegetables.

Sibil made a face as the lights went out and got under the covers. They'd *better* tell her tomorrow.

## 11

## General Kispin's Outer Office

Every seat in the outer office was filled by one of the recruits who had failed the interrogation training exercise.

Gorrak sat opposite the team, nursing his swollen jaw while Sibil fussed around him in an attempt to soothe his bruised ego.

*Talk about ingratitude,* K'aia complained. *I only saved him from being deleted.*

*He'd thank us if he knew he was still breathing because you acted.* Trey grinned at the somewhat nervous looks on the twins' faces as the recruits were called into the inner office in small groups. *Relax. This can't be worse for you than running headlong into live fire. We'll get in there, the general will tell us how stupid we were to act outside of protocol or whatever, and then we can get right back to being run into the ground by the SIs.*

Alexis narrowed her eyes at him. *Look at you, in your comfort zone and showing off your "experience."*

Trey supposed he deserved that. *I apologize for being harsh with you. It was a raw moment, and I behaved badly.*

*It was,* Alexis confirmed stiffly. *And you did.*

Trey tilted his head. *You're doing that thing again where your words and your body language are telling me different things. Is that common among human females?*

Gabriel snorted. *Keep digging* that *hole, and facing the general will be the least of your worries.*

Trey noted Alexis' scowl and shrank back into his seat. *I don't get it. I apologized. Don't you accept it?*

Alexis sighed and unfolded her arms. *I suppose. I'm not going to get bent out of shape because you said something I don't like.*

Gabriel raised an eyebrow. *Since when?*

K'aia waved them down. *Shhh. I can't hear what's going on in there.*

The recruits currently inside the office were getting the dressing down of their lives. They filed out of the office a few moments later, dejected to a one.

The staff sergeant poked her head around the door and fixed the remaining recruits with a glare. "You four." She swept a finger over the outer office to indicate the team. "In here. The general will see you now."

General Kispin sat at his desk, his horn resting on his steepled hands.

Gabriel saw something in the general's pose. He wasn't sure what made him think of his grandfather Lance at that moment, but there it was. He wondered if all generals were short-tempered because their resources had the temerity to come with free will and the ability to mess everything up with a single, thoughtless action.

He had the idea that they were the ones who'd acted thoughtlessly. It wasn't the time for introspection, so he pushed the comparisons aside for later examination.

The general lifted his head and sat straight when the staff sergeant closed the door with a pertinent *snick*.

He cast a frustrated look at the four recruits, who were standing at attention. "At ease. Your unit," he began, "consistently outperforms every other unit in the program. So much so, it skews the unit rankings and gives Sergeant Lokkel a damn headache."

The tight-lipped sergeant nodded to confirm. "I don't mind the headache, sir. These four are Zenith material."

The team looked at each other, confused as to why they were being praised.

General Kispin continued without a sign that he had noticed. "You have all shown leadership skills, courage, and clear thinking in high-pressure situations. You work well with the other recruits, and improve morale wherever you go." He turned his head from side to side, glaring at them around his horn. "So why in the name of all that is fucking right would you attack your superior officers?"

Alexis winced at the slip of language. She raised a hand. "I can explain."

The general jumped to his feet and banged his fist on the desk. "That was rhetorical. This is *my* damned base. I know exactly what occurred, and the officers involved in mistreating recruits are feeling the consequences of their choices. What makes you think I give a shiny shit about your pissant excuses for breaking the chain of command, recruit? This is the *military*, a finely tuned machine of war.

You are not even a cog in it yet. What gives you the impression that you have the right to an opinion?"

Alexis, Gabriel, and K'aia bowed their heads, seeing the truth in the accusation.

Trey had less in the way of self-discipline. "They attacked *us!*" he cried, taking a step toward the desk.

The staff sergeant blocked Trey with a swipe of her arc rod. "Back in line, recruit," she snarled.

Trey held his hands up, stepping back hastily to avoid getting shocked.

General Kispin leaned forward, his raisin eyes all but vanishing under his hooded brow. "Do you think the enemy will ask before attacking? This is what you are training for, recruit. If it wasn't for the fact that you four are the best in the program, I'd throw you all out on your asses and send you back to whatever prison in whatever distant empire you came from."

He sat down again, his earlier calm restored in a blink. "You all have the potential to make something of yourselves—if you decide to put childish pursuits aside and pull on your grown-up pants. Because what I've seen from you all so far, no matter what the sergeant says, not *one* of you is fit for Zenith Squadron."

Alexis groaned internally as the general continued his lecture. *He's right. Sort of. We were so caught up in playing the game that we didn't stop to consider the consequences to our training schedule.*

*We wasted all that time,* Gabriel concurred. *Time we should have spent integrating with our unit.*

Trey nodded. *Well, sure. It would have been good to leave here with a larger group at our backs.*

*How are we going to retrieve this situation?* K'aia asked. *It's gonna suck if we have to start over.*

Gabriel's eyebrow twitched. *Yeah, I wouldn't count on a do-over. Eve only allowed us to reset to the start of an objective chain.*

*You don't get do-overs in real life,* Trey maintained. *That means we'll be going into the next scenario in this chain under-prepared.*

Alexis took charge. *Not if we take it seriously from now on. We grovel, we work our butts off, and we hope to hell we didn't fail the whole objective,* she summarized, raising her hand again. "Permission to speak, sir?"

The general nodded. "You may speak, Female Recruit Nacht," he allowed. "Since you appear to understand protocol after all."

Alexis glanced at the others before standing to attention. "Sir, we apologize as a team for our conduct during the exercise, and for our ingratitude for the opportunity we have been given to fight for the greater good. With your permission, we will make up for our mistakes and ensure our future conduct remains in line with expectations."

The general scrutinized them for a long moment. "Very well. I'm nothing if not fair, so I will give you one chance to prove yourselves." He held up a hand to deny Alexis permission to speak again. "You will retake every exercise and beat your previous efforts. *If*, and that is only if, you do so in a timely manner—say, before the next batch of recruits arrives, we will have another discussion as to your futures as part of this military. Don't let me down again. Do I make myself clear?"

All four saluted General Kispin, feeling slightly more

benevolent toward this more mentorly aspect of him. "Sir, *yes*, sir!"

## Twelve Weeks Later

Trey tried his best not to freak at the sour-tasting rag in his mouth and the rough hands on his body.

The SIs had pulled a sneak attack this time around, bagging the team on the way back from night exercises when they were already at their lowest ebb.

Trey remembered the breathing exercise Gabriel had taught him to bring his heart rate down and he ran through it. In for four, out for three, and repeat until the ringing panic faded enough for his brain to connect to the knowledge that this wasn't what his mother had feared and allow him to hear his team's reassurances.

*We've been training for this*, Gabriel reminded him. *You've got this.*

*Focus on your dissociation techniques*, Alexis added.

K'aia's mind was calm and clear. *Just remember, it's not real. But one day it might be, and lives could depend on your ability to bear what's coming next.*

*How can you be so calm?* Trey asked. His voice was small, even to himself.

K'aia chuckled. *It's not my first interrogation. Physically, we've been through worse than this already. It's all about breaking our minds at this point. Think of it as getting a shot against something much worse. You bear it, and you learn what to expect when the situation happens in real life.*

The SIs took them indoors, then along a short way before turning in different directions.

Trey fought back another wave of panic when the team link went down and he was left alone with his thoughts.

Despite the practice drills they'd done during their limited spare time since restarting the program, he still struggled with a deep-seated phobia of being kidnapped.

The twins empathized, although after hearing their anecdotal retelling of the time they were snatched as small children, Trey didn't think they quite understood what the differences in their early lives and his meant for their contrasting perspectives.

There had been no Addix in his early life to save him. He'd had his mother and Kel'Len. Kel'Len was married to Da'Mahin, but her allegiance was to Mahi', who had raised her. One day, he hoped to hear the tale of how his asshole uncle had been tricked into the union, since the two hated each other.

That was one thing he was grateful for. He might have been an only child, but his mother loved him. His cousins were split in their parents' favor. Ch'Irzt was his father's favorite son, and the others were jealous of their brother's status.

Trey opened his eyes when he was dropped onto a chair and bound around the arms and legs before his hood was removed. He squinted at the slender silhouette of his interrogator against the bright light shining directly into his face. "Hey, you must be my doctor."

He was slapped openhanded across the face hard enough to rattle his teeth. "Four out of ten. My baby cousin has better form. Put some twist into your hip, yeah?"

A distorted voice filled the room, echoing off the close walls. "Who are you working for? Who sent you?"

Trey spat blood on the figure's shoes. "I don't know, but I'm guessing you're not gonna take that for an answer, huh?"

His head rocked back when he was struck again. "Who sent you?"

Trey laughed. K'aia was right; they'd lived through worse than this. They'd trained harder than this. Hells, living with Ch'Irzt was rougher than this…

The warmth he felt at the memory of their last fight surprised him. He couldn't actually be missing his asshole cousins.

Could he?

Trey thought of Mahi' fighting for their home, and of his father, who had died to save them both. Of every day he'd spent using his sharp mind to outwit his scheming uncles and avoid his cousins' beatings.

His mind worked through the list of ways his friends had taught him to mentally step out of the situation, rejecting the human way in favor of being true to himself.

"Who are *you*?" he demanded, taking another slap for his daring. "Because I'll tell you who *I* am. I am Takar'-Tu'Reigd of Qu'Baka and Devon, and I am above anything you can do to me. Hit me again. Go on!"

The interrogator stepped back to avoid Trey's snapping teeth. "Who sent you? What is your purpose?"

Trey offered his cheek, still laughing. "Nobody told you? I'm here to piss you off, you cowardly butt-dribble."

The figure lifted its hood, showing Trey its glowing eyes. "Insolent whelp. You will learn to respect and obey your betters."

Trey felt pain like nothing he had known existed. It

filled him until it felt like his skin would split with the volume of it. The world went gray around him, then another bolt of pain tore through his brain and shocked him to full alertness.

"Clearly you don't know the meaning of the word 'better,'" Trey shot back once the interrogator had torn her mental barbs from his skull.

He glared at the hooded figure, the whites of his eyes bulging as he strained to free himself from the ropes holding him to the chair. "Why don't you untie me and see how long you last?"

Screw this asshole, and every other manipulating asshole who wanted Trey to obey.

All his life, he had put his own feelings aside to take care of Mahi' and her grief. Kept the peace with his cousins to avoid riling their fathers into making a coup attempt. Allowed traditions that kept their people from integrating to continue in the belief that he wasn't capable of making those decisions without a sibling to support him.

No longer.

Trey's head dropped. The comfort of knowing he wasn't alone anymore strengthened his resolve to get through this and anything else his duty threw at him. He had found his family, no matter that they weren't Bakas like him. They believed in his vision for unity, for working together and celebrating what their differences brought to the whole.

He was Takar, and he was done letting anyone tell him to do a damn thing. One day, he would lead Qu'Baka against the Seven, and the twins would lead all who came to them in the Empress' name. Together, they would be unbeatable.

His interrogator leaned in, peering coldly into Trey's eyes. "Who sent you?"

Trey spat blood into his interrogator's face. "Your *mama* sent me. What you gonna do about it?"

## Barracks

Everyone in the room turned when the door was pushed open, flooding the barracks with late morning sun.

Gabriel jumped up as Trey limped in. "Dude. You're back."

Trey glanced at Sibil and Gorrak, the only two NPCs to make it through the final exercise of their basic training. "Am I the last?"

Sibil waved tiredly. "We're advancing to Zenith Squad. The announcement went out about an hour ago." She groaned as she turned on her bed to face the others. "I hope we get a couple more days rest, first. That was brutal."

Gorrak scoffed, the sound muffled by his swollen jaw. "It was nothing."

Alexis dashed over to wrap Trey in a hug. "We were getting worried. You've been gone for two days!"

"Two days?" Trey grimaced. "Felt like a lot longer than that." He winced, extracting himself from Alexis' arms. "Easy on the ribs. I'm still healing."

K'aia inspected Trey's body as he walked by. Her eyes widened as she counted the new scars where his fur hadn't grown back yet. "Good gods, what did they put you through?"

"Enough to make sure I've got the scars of a true warrior." Trey slid gently onto his bunk, being careful not to aggravate his healing injuries. "But I'm healing fast. Faster than I should be. Looks like another ability got unlocked."

Alexis grinned, her eyes shining with relief. "Eve must have been forced to accelerate the process. You look like you spent the last two days in a rock-washer."

Gabriel had a thought. "The scarring probably won't transfer to your real body."

Trey lifted his head, regretting it when the torn muscles in his neck and upper back complained. "They'd better be on my real body! I didn't just spend two days taunting that asshole to leave here with no scars to show for it."

Gabriel knew Trey had been worried about lacking the Bakas' marks of courage. "You told Eve to leave your scarring alone, right?"

Trey eased himself onto his pillow. "Didn't think to. I'm hoping she's listening."

Alexis shrugged. "We'll see." She settled back with her arms folded behind her head. "I'm glad we've gotten downtime after that exercise."

"Yeah," Gabriel agreed. "How did you do, Trey? Did they get anything out of you?"

Trey snorted. "They learned how annoying a pissed-off Baka can be. That's about it. I just thought about Mahi', and how I'm strong like she taught me to be. That got me through it."

Alexis turned to climb onto her bunk. "You can always send her a message. Have you worked out your internal HUD yet?"

Trey's eyebrows met in the middle. "I've got a what, now?"

Alexis raised an eyebrow. "Very funny, Trey." Her laughter dried up when she saw he wasn't joking. "It came with your neural chip. Didn't you follow the prompts after you had the procedure?"

Trey dropped his pretense and burst out laughing. "Of course, I did. I'm not a complete dumbass. Eve heard me, I know it. She doesn't need me to bother her with messages."

Gabriel felt a tingle in his mind. He frowned at the unexpected sensation, and then the notification came up in his HUD. "I've got a message."

Alexis sat bolt upright as she was hit by the same sensation. "I got it too."

"What is Eve saying?" K'aia asked. She poked her head out of her bunk to get a view of Gabriel.

"It's not from Eve," Alexis clarified. "It's from Mom and Dad. Gabriel, I don't like this. I got the worst feeling when I opened the message."

Trey eased himself into a sitting position, ignoring his physical pain. "Your 'feelings' are never wrong, Alexis." He hesitated to ask why he hadn't received a message from Mahi'. "What did they say?"

Gabriel hopped down from his bunk and grabbed his boots from under the bed. "They're coming into the game to talk to us."

K'aia had an idea about what would make Bethany Anne and Michael interrupt their training, and it wasn't anything good. "Something's wrong."

Alexis pursed her lips. "Well, yeah. Otherwise, I'd have gotten a happy psychic flash instead of the ocean of sorrow that drowned me for a second." She fixed K'aia with a concerned look. "We'll be back soon."

Gabriel touched Alexis' arm as he set off for the door. "We'd better go."

The rest of the day crawled by for Trey and K'aia.

Trey slept some. He also wrote to Mahi', a long letter full of longing for home and her presence. There was no sign of Alexis and Gabriel returning to the barracks.

K'aia spent the time maintaining her carapace. She held back her rebukes for Trey's restlessness, feeling the same nervous tension of not knowing what the bad news was. It was up to her as the eldest to ensure all three had support.

There wasn't much she hadn't lived through during her time as a slave in the salt mine. She was tougher than all three, having spent the majority of her life with no status whatsoever.

K'aia enjoyed the luxury of having people around her who cared, but she never let herself forget what it had been to be owned.

The twins would return, and then they would tell her what loss they'd suffered. Whatever the emotional fallout, she would be there the way her duty to them as a friend demanded. Same thing with Trey. It couldn't be easy knowing your only parent was away at war and might not make it back.

She couldn't see Bethany Anne achieving anything except victory, but what price had fate charged for it?

Fate always called in her chits.

K'aia buffed out the scratches in her carapace and kept her counsel to herself.

The dinner bell rang, and K'aia made Trey hobble over

to the mess tent. They ate their mush in strained silence, neither wanting to put a name to the cloud hanging over their heads.

It was full dark when Gabriel and Alexis finally came back to the barracks. They trooped in together, the dejection surrounding them almost physical in its presence.

Trey dropped the book he was reading and sat up on his mattress. "What is it?"

Alexis burst into tears. "I...I can't!" She ran into one of the bathrooms and shut the door.

Gabriel was in little better shape. He climbed up to his bunk without saying a word.

K'aia hesitated, torn between them. She settled on Trey, who looked confounded. "Stay with Gabriel."

Alexis didn't reply when K'aia tapped on the bathroom door. She tapped again. "Alexis? What happened?"

There was a *snick* as Alexis unlocked the door. She opened it, then hopped up onto the cistern and rested her feet on the toilet lid to make room for K'aia. "Come in."

K'aia was less than certain about the wisdom of trying to fit both her and Alexis into a bathroom made for one. "Just come out. There's no point you being in there. There's no one here to see you cry but us."

Alexis sighed, but did as K'aia asked. "I just wanted to be alone for a minute is all. Addix. She's dead."

K'aia's heart dropped. "No." She turned to see Trey receiving the news from Gabriel. "Not Addix. She's too tough to die!"

Alexis nodded, fresh tears flowing without her noticing. "Yes. There was an Ooken; it had Mahi'. She saved Mahi', but she didn't survive."

K'aia couldn't believe what she was hearing, but she wasn't as shaken as the others. Sad, yes, but she had spent long hours considering the role of a bodyguard and whether she could fill it before agreeing to Bethany Anne and Michael's request to protect the twins.

Addix had made it clear in their first lesson that there weren't many retired bodyguards to be found, outside of the fully enhanced. K'aia expected to lay down her life one day if that was the only way she could keep the twins safe.

Perhaps she shouldn't have been so eager to refuse the extra enhancement.

K'aia embraced Alexis, her own grief pushed to the side for the moment. "I'm sorry you lost Addix. She was an aunt to you and Gabriel during a huge part of your lives."

Alexis returned the hug, uncaring of the pain hugging a Yollin caused. "She was your mentor and your friend. You two spent a lot of time together." She paused to place a hand on Trey's shoulder before taking a seat on K'aia's bunk. "Are you okay?"

Trey held his head in his hands. He looked at Alexis through his fingers. "I don't know what to feel. I can't believe Addix sacrificed herself. I also can't imagine life without Mahi'. I'm grateful, but I wish it hadn't been necessary."

K'aia smiled sadly. "That was her duty. One day I might have to do the same for one of you. That's life."

"No, it isn't," Alexis argued. "Nobody has to die. Not when we have the technology to make everyone invulnerable."

Gabriel frowned. "It's not that easy. You know what happens when it gets out that the tech exists. Riots amongst the people, and attacks we have to fend off by those who can afford to send their militaries after us. War. Mom keeps a tight grip on our technology for a reason."

Alexis glared at him. "I'm talking about K'aia getting fully enhanced so she doesn't die protecting us," she ground out. "I'm not asking. K'aia, either you get level-three enhancement, or we get a new bodyguard. I will *not* risk you."

K'aia knew Alexis spoke from a place of fear. "I'll think about it. What about Addix? Did we miss her funeral?"

Gabriel shook his head. "No. It's in three weeks game-time. Mom instructed us to complete this objective chain in that time, and told us we'll be placed into the next scenario when we get back from the funeral."

## 12

**Devon, The Hexagon, Penthouse Apartment, Roof Terrace**

Bethany Anne stepped back as the casket representing Addix was fired into Devon's star. There was a brief flash as the BYPS allowed the casket passage, and then it was gone.

Alexis slipped away from Bethany Anne and Gabriel, feeling the need for some quiet to work through the growing anger that had built up over the last three weeks.

Trey thought about offering her his shoulder until he saw her eyes were glowing again. She was raging inside, and he knew there was nothing he could do to ease the pain of a lost relative.

He glanced around and spotted his mother talking to a Baka he didn't recognize. He drifted away from the attendees and walked over to the wall. "Mahi', I wondered where you were when we got out of the Vid-docs."

Mahi' turned and stared open-mouthed at him for a moment before speaking. "Tu'Reigd? Is that you?" She limped over and wrapped Trey in a tight hug. "I'm not cleared for the vault since Tabitha upped the security. Even Bethany Anne and Michael had to wait for it to be disabled before they were able to visit."

She stood on her tiptoes and cupped Trey's face in her hands. "Look how handsome you are, all grown. You're the image of your father, but I always knew you would be."

Trey bent gratefully into his mother's embrace, for once not embarrassed by the public display of affection. "It's so good to see you, even though it's for a sad occasion. All I've wanted to do since you wrote to me about Qu'Baka is hug you."

Mahi' released him and stepped back, taking her weight on her good leg. "You came close to losing me, but we did not lose our people, and the Seven were unable to do more than take their frustration out on the planet. Addix's sacrifice will be remembered forever." Her expression was tight and sad. "She was a good friend, as well as a warrior of unimpeachable honor. This celebration of her life is apt."

Trey dropped his gaze to her leg. "Michael told me an Ooken took your leg. How are you doing with the prosthetic? You could have it regrown, no one would judge you for it. Except for Da'Mahin, but who listens to him, anyway?"

Mahi' smiled and shook her head fondly. "Always concerned about others. I'll get used to my new leg, and it will serve to remind me always of Addix's sacrifice." Her smile grew wider as linked her arm through Trey's and steered them both toward the wall, where the Baka Mahi' had been talking to stood looking out over First City. "Besides, can you see Da'Mahin topping my lost leg? We'll see who has the most gripping war story at the next family gathering. Come with me. There's someone special I want you to meet."

Trey found that his curiosity was piqued by the unknown Baka. Golden fur was as rare among their people as truly red hair in humans. He was sure he would have noticed a Baka so large walking around the Enclave. By that reasoning, this must be a relative Mahi' had found on Qu'Baka. "Is he your uncle? Bor'Dane?"

Mahi' shook her head, tears transforming her eyes into mirrors. "No, Bor'Dane is at the Enclave at the moment. We rescued many political prisoners when we freed our people." She repressed a sob. "When our home was lost."

Trey couldn't stand to see his mother hurting. "Devon is our home. We will build a new Citadel, a bigger one, with no access for Da'Mahin unless he asks really, really nicely."

Mahi' offered Trey a smile for his efforts. "You are a good son." She let go of Trey and put a hand on the stranger's arm. "Fi', look who's here!"

The mystery Baka abandoned his lookout to smile at Mahi', then at Trey. "This must be… I'm not sure. Let me guess, Li'Orin?"

Trey held out a hand, no clearer on who this relative was, but amused by the mistake. "Hi. Um, no. I'm Tu'Reigd. Good to meet you, Fi'… What is your name?"

The Baka clasped Trey's forearm in a strong grip. "Fi'Eireie." He grinned at Trey's response to his name. "Good to know you haven't forgotten me. Hello, son."

Trey looked into tawny eyes identical to his own and it hit him. "Father? No. Freaking. Way. You're alive?"

Fi'Eireie patted himself down. "Last time I checked. What has your mother been feeding you? Hells, you're taller than me! The last time I saw you, you barely reached my knee."

Alexis watched the reunion with mixed emotions. This was the reason Addix had given her life—so Trey's family could be together.

It didn't hurt any less to know she would never see her Ixtali aunt again.

Who could she blame? She *needed* someone to blame. Some focus for the anger she felt at the early theft of a person she loved. Not Mahi', and definitely not Addix herself. The Ooken that had attacked was no more than a mindless creature under Kurtherian control. Where did the responsibility lie?

Ultimately, Alexis knew it was with the Seven. She burned with the urge to take revenge, but what could she do? They weren't ready for that fight.

Gabriel dropped into the seat next to Alexis, his face as solemn as the cut of the white suit he wore. "I can feel you stewing from inside the apartment. Wanna talk?"

Alexis pressed her lips together and wrapped her arms around her drawn-up legs. "No, I want to wipe the Seven from existence. It's not difficult to understand Mom's focus on making that day come around soonest." Her face settled into a harsh grimace. "I'm sick of being stuck halfway between childhood and the rest of our lives. We need to prepare ourselves for facing the Seven."

K'aia joined them, working out the subject easily. "We have to get back into the Vid-docs and complete our enhancement."

Trey ran over. "You'll never guess. That Baka, the one with Mahi'? He's my father!" He waved down their congratulations. "You don't understand. With my father around, he and Mahi' control enough of the people to shut my uncles out. Our troubles as a people are over."

Alexis raised an eyebrow. "What does that mean for you?"

Trey lifted a shoulder. "It means I'm free for the moment. I still have to rule, just not while my parents are here to do it. Right now, I want to get vengeance for Addix."

"We will," Alexis assured him. "The minute we're ready."

Gabriel had been thinking along the same lines. He glanced at their parents, seeing them in deep discussion with Eve and Ashur. "We'll be there soon enough. All of us."

**Devon, The Hexagon, Vid-doc Vault**

The atmosphere was muted inside the vault as the Vid-docs were prepared to reinsert the team at the moment they had left the game to attend Addix's funeral.

K'aia had little to say beyond expressing her desire to get back into the program. The decision to take level-three enhancement had not been easy to come to.

Alexis touched Gabriel's mind. *Whatever it takes, I want us to be ready to fight when we get back.*

*We will be,* Gabriel promised. *Zenith Squad is where we'll get those skills, and Belv'th is where we're going to hone them.*

Trey resisted the urge to tell his parents he wanted to stay with them. He embraced Mahi' and Fi'Eireie, tears threatening his hard-won composure.

Fi'Eireie took him by the shoulders, pride shining in his eyes. "I could not be more honored by the son you have been to your mother, or by the dedication you have to our people. I see wisdom despite your youth, and I see the marks of your courage on your body."

Trey nodded, finding it hard to say goodbye to the father he'd only just gotten to know. "Look after Mahi' for me. Make sure Da'Mahin doesn't give her any more trouble."

Mahi' held Trey close, then released him and traced the path of the scar on his cheek with her thumb. "You are too young to have borne this already. You experienced every one of these injuries, it doesn't matter that your scars were created by Eve. You are not obligated to complete this, Tu'Reigd. Your father and I are here to take care of the people."

Trey shook his head, resolved to his choice. "I'm going to finish. You are here for our people, and I have a higher calling to answer. My fight is with the Seven now." He put a hand on his mother's cheek. "This is what I have to do. It's just a few months more. In your time, anyway."

Mahi' nodded solemnly. "I understand. Fight well, my son. We will be here waiting when you return."

Alexis was about to climb into her Vid-doc when Bethany Anne stopped her with a touch on her arm. "Mom?"

"I want to tell you something before you leave. You too, Gabriel." Bethany Anne took Alexis by the hand. "Let that anger go. There's no gain in hating the Kurtherians."

Alexis looked at her mother in disbelief. "You can't be serious? The Seven ruin everything!"

"I'm deadly serious," Bethany Anne told her in a firm tone. "It will destroy you if you hold onto it. Be angry, yes, but don't let it fester and grow until that's all you are."

Gabriel frowned. "I don't get it. I can feel your

emotions, Mom. You're beyond angry. Why shouldn't we be angry too? Our aunt was killed in cold blood."

Bethany Anne gave them a small smile. "My babies. This is our life, and our enemies will take any chance they can to hurt us." She turned as Michael joined them, not pausing in her lesson. "My mentor was killed just for knowing me. Your father has been through worse. At every turn since, I have had to protect myself and the people I care about from attacks. If I allowed my emotions to rule me, none of us would be here."

Michael nodded to confirm Bethany Anne's words. "We have had lifetimes to learn the difference between right-eous anger and the kind you are feeling right now. It is my hope that we have prepared you to recognize it too before you end up on a path you regret."

"You're not the only ones with a grudge to settle," Bethany Anne added. "Never forget what was taken, but do not allow your emotions to be your downfall."

Alexis exchanged a glance with her brother, knowing that it was her temper that put them at risk of failure. "I'll do my best. It's not easy to let go."

Gabriel nodded. "But we've got each other to make sure neither of us falls," he told Bethany Anne.

"We're going to make a difference," Alexis vowed. "We are going to face the Seven as a family." She climbed into her Vid-doc, her anger transformed into a cold shard she stuffed down inside to save for when that moment came.

Gabriel followed suit. He paused before lying down on the neural mat. "We're going to focus on becoming the best we can be. You're right, anger will get in the way. But it can also be a tool."

Alexis picked up as Gabriel lay back. "Be prepared for when we return, because we're coming out ready to kick Kurtherian ass from one side of the universe to the other if that's what it requires to make sure they can't take anything from anyone ever again."

Bethany Anne glanced at Michael as the Vid-docs' lids closed. "They're determined to join this war."

Michael put his arm around Bethany Anne's shoulders. "We raised them that way. We should have known the day would come when the Seven became their focus too." He smiled at her. "I'm proud of them. They had the choice of any life they wanted, and they chose the fight for what's right."

"Whatever their future, they are everything they need to be to tackle it head-on." Bethany Anne's mouth turned up at the corner. "I just hope the universe is equipped to handle the waves they're going to make."

Thank you for joining Alexis and Gabriel on the first steps of their journey into adulthood, and thank you even *more* for staying to read this note!

Isn't it good to get a look at the twins at last! I'm quite sure everyone has seen K'aia and Trey as well, but for those who haven't, here are the artworks made by Eric Quigley for the Endgame series.

*K'aia*

*Trey*

I have a thousand more thank-yous to say. First, to my family and friends, whose love and support I couldn't live without. To everyone who made my world by being so excited that this book was coming! To everyone who worked to make sure this book reached readers with a minimum of oopsies. To Andrew Dobell for the beautiful cover.

Last but not least, to Michael for being so abundantly imaginative that I keep having to write more books. If you missed the story of how this series came to be, it's here in this post from my Facebook page, where I can be found sporadically waffling between writing binges.

https://www.facebook.com/NDRobertsBooks/
posts/2052879758339966

I like to hop around and explore different genres while I'm helping to fill out other parts of the Kurtherian time-line, like the Age of Madness, but my favorite thing to write is actually the smaller stories, especially those defining moments in a character's life that shape them to make the big decisions.

There's nothing more defining than the short time between adolescence and adulthood, and as a parent I'm learning that at first the change happens in lots of little stages. Then all at once you notice—oh, my goodness, you grew up!

Does this count as parenting Bethany Anne's children? I hope not, those two are far too clever for me! I'll settle for guiding them, and that's only going to get more chal-lenging as they get further into the game. I have faith in the team finding a whole lot more trouble when they step up a level.

I wonder what kind of challenge Zenith Squad will be for them? I'm sure I'll find out in the coming weeks, and I can't wait to share the next part of the story with you!

Until the next book,

Nat

Thank you for reading this book, AND these author notes!

In less than a couple of months, we will celebrate the fourth anniversary of *Death Becomes Her* being released. There was no way I could have foreseen what that book (and the ones that came after) would accomplish, and how they would be the catalyst for such change in so many lives.

For example, four years ago, I certainly had NO idea who Natale Roberts was, nor had I ever visited her country (England).

Now, four years later, we have collaborated on a good number of stories, and we have even met in both London at 20Booksto50k® events there and at the 20Booksto50k® Vegas event here in the US.

Plus, more importantly, Bethany Anne has KIIDDSSS.

When I first created Bethany Anne, my intention was that she wouldn't get married, much less get married and have kids.

I went so far as to kill off her boyfriend Michael to

make sure I never had to worry about her significant other getting in the way of the story being about her, not *them*.

We see what that decision cost me...a whole quartet of books to get him back and saying, "I'm sorry" to a few hundred fans who practically threw their Kindles against the wall, when they didn't throw them at me. I've no idea how many readers I lost with that one decision.

I won't do it again. Nope, *significant others do not get killed*.

Maybe...*perhaps*... Well, let's say, I won't promise, but I WILL think really long and really hard before ever doing something like that again.

So, when it became obvious that Bethany Anne's kids were either going to be in the war or something needed to be done with them, it was a fairly straightforward decision.

"Do I want to be realistic and believe I can put them in harm's way as teenagers and they never get hurt / dead...or do I grow them up?"

One was not going to happen, so the other was a good call. ;-)

So was asking Natale for her help on these stories.

Fortunately, Natale has a teenager of her own (I'm a few years after empty nest, so my memory of teenagers is questionable at best. I try to forget the horrible stuff in my life.)

Natale and I hope you enjoy the decision Bethany Anne made as her children work their way towards...

MATURITY.

Pre-order now to have the book arrive on your Kindle November 1st.

**Two Rebels whose Worlds Collide on a Planetary Level.**
**On the fringes of human space, a murder will light a fuse and send two different people colliding together.**

She lives on Earth, where peace among the population is a given. He is on the fringe of society where authority is how much firepower you wield.

*She is from the powerful, the elite. He is with the military.*

**Both want the truth – but is revealing the truth good for society?**

---

**Two years ago, a small moon in a far off system was set to be the location of the first intergalactic war between humans and an alien race.**

It never happened. However, something was found many are willing to kill to keep a secret.

*Now, they have killed the wrong people.*

How many will need to die to keep the truth hidden?

*As many as is needed.*

**He will have vengeance no matter the cost.** *She will dig for the truth. No matter how risky the truth is to reveal.*

Coming November 1st from Amazon and other Digital Book Stores

## CONNECT WITH MICHAEL ANDERLE

**Michael Anderle Social**
  **Website:**
  http://www.lmbpn.com

**Email List:**
  http://lmbpn.com/email/

**Facebook Here:**
  www.facebook.com/TheKurtherianGambitBooks/